MW01148240

BOUND BY
A PROMISE

ALEATHA ROMIG
NEW YORK TIMES BESTSELLING AUTHOR

Book #3 of the Brutal Vows series

Aleatha Romig

New York Times, Wall Street Journal, and USA Today
bestselling author

COPYRIGHT AND LICENSE INFORMATION

ALEATHA ROMIG'S MOST RECENT AND UPCOMING RELEASES

QUEENS AND MONSTERS - Brutal Vows, book four - Coming 2025

BOUND BY A PROMISE – Brutal Vows, book three - October 2024

Arranged marriage, age-gap, forbidden, mafia/cartel stand-alone romance

ONE STRING – July 2024

Aleatha's Lighter Ones - Second-chance, enemies-to-lovers, fake-date, little-sister's-best-friend, forbidden, stand-alone contemporary romance

NOW AND FOREVER – Brutal Vows, book one - May 2024

Arranged marriage, age-gap, mafia/cartel stand-alone romance

LIGHT DARK – April 2024

Cult, psychological thriller, forced proximity, romantic suspense stand-alone

*Previously published through Thomas and Mercer as INTO THE LIGHT and AWAY FROM THE DARK

REMEMBERING PASSION – Sinclair Duet book one – September 2023

Scorching hot, second-chance romance filled with the suspense and intrigue

REKINDLING DESIRE – Sinclair Duet, book two – October 2023

Scorching hot, second-chance romance filled with the suspense and intrigue

For a complete list of all Aleatha Romig's works, turn to BOOKS BY ALEATHA at the end of this novel.

SYNOPSIS:

Arranged-marriage, age-gap, Mafia/cartel romance, forbidden

Due to my birth order as a child of the Luciano famiglia capo, I'm used to second place.

Second son.

Second in standing.

Never number one.

It's the way my life has always been.

Only in the dark alleys, private clubs, and seedy establishments am I respected. Not just as the consigliere to my brother, the new capo of the Kansas City Famiglia, but also for my unmatched skills with a knife and my particular skills of interrogation. This status is as high as I will achieve. First place will forever be out of reach.

Camila Ruiz is the younger daughter of Andrés Ruiz, a top lieutenant in the Roríguez cartel. From the first moment I laid eyes on her, I knew I wanted her. She is too young and fragile, though, to be with a man like me, a killer and criminal. I don't deserve a woman like Camila. Taking her would ruin her.

With the newly established alliance between the Luciano famiglia and Roríguez cartel, I ask for the impossible and promise my life. With the blessing of my capo and the Roríguez drug lord, Camila is to be mine.

For once, I will be first in another's eyes. And Camila will always be first to me.

What happens when the fragile alliance is tested?
    Can I keep my promise to my wife and my oath to the famiglia?

Have you been Aleatha'd?

BOUND BY A PROMISE is a stand-alone dangerous Mafia/cartel romance in the interconnected world of the "Brutal Vows" series. Each arranged-marriage story is filled with the suspense, intrigue, and heat you've come to expect from New York Times best-selling author Aleatha Romig.

PROLOGUE

Dante

Summer in the Ozark Mountains

T he door to my bedroom suite opened without the benefit of a knock. Under normal circumstances, I would have my gun pointed at the intruder. Tonight wasn't normal circumstances. It was the eve of my only brother's wedding. Dario was the person entering my suite. Shooting the future groom wouldn't be a great way to begin the festivities. Instead, I lifted the decanter of bourbon I'd procured from our father's supply on the first floor of this mansion. Our father wouldn't miss the Blanton's Silver Edition Single Barrel, not with the ample supply of liquor at his fingertips.

"You missed your rehearsal dinner," I said with an

upward twitch of my lips. "I was beginning to think you'd miss this rambunctious bachelor party."

Dario hummed as he looked around the living area of my suite, empty of people other than us. "My kind of party."

"You never did know how to have fun." Standing, I walked the decanter to the makeshift bar and poured two fingers of the amber liquid into two tumblers.

With his tie and suit coat absent, this was my brother's idea of casual. Despite his lack of formality, the stress and pressure of the last few months was difficult to disguise. It was evident in the tenseness of his jaw and the small lines near his dark eyes.

I handed him a glass and lifted mine. "To the groom."

Our glasses clinked.

The two fingers of Blanton's slid down my throat with ease. Of course, this wasn't my first drink of the night. It wasn't even my third, but I wasn't counting. I slammed my tumbler onto the table as Dario set his empty glass down and sighed.

"You found the good stuff," he said, pouring another shot into each glass.

"I saw her, your bride, tonight at dinner."

Dario shook his head. "I should have fucking been there."

I nodded my agreement. "I got the feeling she was looking for you."

"Father had a fire, literally."

I lifted my eyebrows in question.

"Shipping container," Dario went on, "went up in smoke."

2

My stomach turned. "Contents?"

"Product, not the humankind. We probably lost fifteen million in product." My brother shook his head. "Father thinks it's the bratva."

"You don't?"

"None of Myshkin's usual calling cards were there. The night before my wedding to a woman from the Roríguez cartel...Maybe I'm paranoid, but I think it was meant as a warning."

"Not to go through with the wedding?" I straightened my neck. "Not from our people."

"I wouldn't rule anyone out."

My brother took his glass to one of the overstuffed armchairs near the fireplace and sat back, stretching out his long legs. "As for the bride, she found me." His lips curled almost enough for a grin. "Or we found her."

After sitting in the chair near him, I asked, "What? When?"

"A few minutes ago," he said. "In the kitchen. Catalina was down there looking for something to eat." He lifted his glass to his lips.

When he didn't continue, I prompted, "And..." My thought was that it would be easier to pull teeth than get Dario to talk. I'd pulled my share. It would be easier. "You don't have to be so forthcoming with the information."

Dario shrugged. "No information. We talked. Something I should have tried to do earlier than the night before our wedding." He swirled the amber liquid in his tumbler.

"You should have. You've kind of been an ass to her."

3

"I haven't been anything to her." He set his glass on the table. "Ever since the engagement, Father's had me running in all directions. The famiglia will burn to the ground if he doesn't step down and soon."

Once word made it onto the streets about our famiglia's alliance with the Roríguez cartel, we've been bombarded from all sides. Our father's quick temper hadn't quelled the rising temperatures within the famiglia or between different organizations. My thoughts went back to Dario's bride. "Did she tell you off?"

"No. I have the feeling she understands what her father, brother, and uncles do. It's not too difficult to understand what's been occupying my time."

"She's beautiful," I admitted. "If she's understanding as well, you might have hit the jackpot. But..." I elongated the last word.

Dario lifted his eyebrows.

"You had your choice, right?"

"I chose Catalina. You know that."

"What about her sister?"

"Camila?"

I nodded, my pulse increasing at the sound of her name.

My brother's forehead furrowed. "Camila is a child."

She didn't look like a child to me.

Dario went on, "The last thing I want to do is marry a child. This alliance is going to require delicate diplomacy. I don't have the time or energy to raise a wife." He shook his head. "Catalina has proven herself to be self-reliant, with her education. She won't need to be instructed at every turn."

Giving that some thought, I let my cheeks rise in a grin. "Jorge promised she's pure. Some instruction will be needed."

Dario's lips pressed together. "I'm not talking about sex. I'm talking about life."

On a good day, my brother was hard to read. With all that was happening, tonight wouldn't be classified as good. His expression was impenetrable.

"I know her virginity isn't an issue for you. It is for Mother."

Dario's dark eyes narrowed. "Her purity isn't to be questioned even by you."

I lifted my hand in surrender. "I'm just saying, you didn't care about virginity when it came to Josie."

My brother and I have always been close, but broaching the subject of Josie was a stretch even for me. "Sorry," I said, flashing a smile. "My bad. It's just that the younger one caught my eye. I've been thinking..."

"Stop thinking. She's going to college and way too fucking young for you."

Dario was probably right. And even if he wasn't, as the soon-to-be-named capo, any relationship I'd want to pursue with Camila would be at his discretion. It was good I wasn't looking for a relationship. Dario could cement the alliance with his marriage. That should be enough.

The following afternoon I stood at Dario's side in our parents' garden and scanned the unlikely gathering. With the Mafia on one side of the aisle and the cartel on the other, tension rippled through the air, almost visible in waves shimmering within the summer breeze. The earlier show of surrendering weapons upon entry was only that—a performance. Personally, I still had two guns and two knives. Knowing my brother, he was carrying even more weapons. All it would take was an itchy trigger finger to turn this wedding into a bloodbath.

My attention went to the woman walking down the aisle—the one Dario proclaimed as too young. Standing statuesque, my gaze lingered on her slender figure, partially hidden beneath the bridesmaid dress. The neckline dipped just enough to expose the top of her tiny breasts. Her long dark hair was secured on the sides and hanging in waves over her shoulders. The color of the dress intensified her emerald-green eyes, the ones I'd noticed last night.

The congregation stood as the music changed. An audible gasp of appreciation sounded from the rows of guests as my soon-to-be sister-in-law stood at the end of the aisle, her hand on her father's arm.

As Dario took Catalina's hand, I wondered if I was attracted to the younger Ruiz, or if as in most of my life, I was second to my older brother. Was his wedding making me think of my own? The thought that I was interested in anything other than a casual encounter almost made me laugh. I successfully let my mind concentrate on my brother and his bride and the current lack of bloodshed, that was, until it was time to walk back down the aisle. As best man, I was paired with the maid of honor.

Camila smiled up at me as we approached one another before gently laying her petite hand on my arm. The fragrance of cinnamon filled my senses. Seeing her fragile fingers, slender wrists...Dario was right. Camila was too young. More than that, she was too delicate to be with a man like me. Swallowing, I nodded with a grin of indifference as we paraded toward the back of the makeshift aisle.

CHAPTER

ONE

Camila
Almost a year later

The piercing whine of alarms ripped me from my sleep. Opening my eyes wide to the darkness of my bedroom, I scanned the corners as my pulse thumped in my veins. Strobing lights flashed beneath the bottom edge of my door, giving my bedroom the eerie feeling of a Halloween haunted house. Yet within, nothing seemed out of place.

My mind scrambled for answers.

Alarms meant intruders.

While other children were told stories of princesses and princes or perhaps adventures with dragon riders, from an early age, our father's stories warned my siblings and me of dangers in the real world. There weren't happily-ever-afters in his tales. His honesty wasn't meant to scare us as much as it was to prepare us.

His affiliation with the Roríguez cartel as a top lieutenant put a target on our backs. That was why when my siblings and I were younger, we were constantly watched over by our bodyguards. Now that we're adults, for my sister and me, the rules hadn't changed. While Catalina's bodyguards were with her in Kansas City, Miguel remained in San Diego with me. He'd been at my side for most of my memory. My brother Emiliano no longer needed protection. Like our bodyguards, our brother was an effective killing machine. That wasn't what I saw when I sat across the dining room table; nevertheless, it was the truth. In our world, killing was too common.

Is someone trying to kill us?

My hands trembled and my ears rang as I pulled a hooded sweatshirt over my sleeping shorts and camisole. The decal on the front displayed the letters SDSU, San Diego State University. I'd recently finished my first year.

Contemplating the idea that I may not live to see my second year, I held my breath and searched my room for a weapon as the door to my bedroom swung inward.

"Camila," Miguel said, his voice barely audible above the alarms. He lowered his gun and rushed toward me. "*Apúrese.*"

"What's happening?"

"Russians. We're getting you and your mother to the safe room."

He reached for my hand.

His grip was a vise.

My mother and me. What about the others? "Em?" I

asked. When Miguel didn't answer, I raised my volume over the screaming alarms. "Is he okay?"

"*Sí. Ven.*"

I stared up into the dark orbs of the man I'd known most of my life. Miguel was my father's employee, but he was more than that to me. While he was deadly accurate with a shot, I knew him as the man who drank imaginary tea at my tea parties when I was young. He not only watched over me as I swam but taught me to swim. Our blood wasn't shared, but he was a part of my family. "Are we safe?"

"My job is you. I won't let anything happen to you."

"Or you."

The howl of the alarm shrilled louder in the hallway as I walked crouched behind my bodyguard. I hesitated as he led me away from the front staircase and away from my parents' wing of the house. "What about Mama?"

"Luis is with her."

Luis Bosco was the head of our family's security. I couldn't recall a time when he wasn't present. Like Miguel, he was more family than employee.

As we traveled along the wall, moving toward the back stairs, I remembered the second wedding cementing the Roriguez cartel and Luciano famiglia's alliance, of Aléjandro Roriguez and Mia Luciano, that had taken place in this home only a few days before. The fierce contrast from then to now made my skin prickle.

Suddenly, the house went dark and deadly quiet. The abrupt change left my head reeling. Miguel stopped walking as the new silence enveloped us, seeming somehow louder than the alarms.

"Fuck," he mumbled. "They cut the power."

"How?"

Instead of answering, Miguel continued moving toward the back steps with his gun drawn. He lowered his voice. "Stay close."

At the bottom of the stairs, Miguel stretched out his arm, keeping me in place. I held my breath as I watched red lines of light crisscross through our kitchen. The safe room was in the lower level. The only way to the next set of stairs was through the kitchen.

"Get down."

My bodyguard, over six feet of muscle, was on his hands and knees. I quickly followed. Together we crawled, keeping our heads below the streaming lights. I wasn't certain if I remembered to breathe until we made it to the second staircase. It was as we began the descent that we heard a scream.

I knew that voice.

Tears filled my eyes as I reached for Miguel. "Mama."

We both stayed immobile waiting for another sound. Only silence followed.

My stomach twisted as tears slid down my cheeks. "Is she...?" I couldn't say the word. My mother couldn't be dead. "You need to go to her."

"Not until you're safe."

"Please."

"Ven," he said again, telling me to come.

I was torn between wanting to find my mother and fearing for my life. The pops of fireworks echoed from beyond the glass doors leading to our pool deck. Specks of light flashed in the darkness. In my heart I knew the noises and flashes weren't coming from the fireworks of an early celebration. The sounds I heard and the pops of light I saw were gunshots.

Gunshots right outside the glass doors.

For a split second, I thought about Rei Roríguez, the son of the cartel's leader, Jorge. Rei had been living in our pool house for a while. If he were here, he'd help. I then remembered that he wasn't here but out on the Bella, *el Patron's* yacht.

The next few moments occurred in slow motion or maybe it was my lack of sufficient breathing. I couldn't fill my lungs as my breaths came fast and shallow. Crouching low, Miguel led me toward the safety of our secret room. As he entered the combination of numbers into the keypad, the glass doors behind us shattered.

A monstrous explosion of glass and sound.

I covered my face from the flying shards.

Miguel pushed me down, landing on top of me as my home erupted in gunshots.

I looked up as Miguel's fingers pressed the numbers. The keypad didn't light.

"Where's the generator?" Miguel cursed. His head turned in every direction. "Come."

Crawling along the floor, he led me back into the lower level, toward the sauna. The all-wood room was smaller than those found in a spa. After opening the door, he used the flashlight on his phone to scan the room. "Go and hide under the benches," he ordered.

Sitting up on my knees, I froze, taking in the empty

room. My pulse beat in double time at the dark, secluded space. "What about Mama?"

"I'll find her. Stay down and don't make a sound." He reached for my shoulders. "If someone enters, stay as quiet as possible."

Holding back the bile percolating in my stomach, I did as Miguel said and again lowered myself to my stomach, crawling to the darkest corner and scooting beneath the lowest bench. I pulled my knees up to my chest and under the dark hoodie. Lying with my back against the wall, I tucked my arms inside my sweatshirt and stared through the darkness in the direction of the door.

Through the inky darkness, I heard the door close.

Seconds later the popping of gunfire erupted beyond my bubble. Even from the depths of the lower level, my body trembled with the rapid succession of bullets.

Reaching for my phone, I realized I'd left it plugged in back in my bedroom. I had no way to communicate, to call for help, or to even know the time of night. I also didn't have a way to distinguish how much time passed.

When the barrage of bullets finally stopped, I lay perfectly still, afraid to breathe as I stared wide-eyed toward the door.

What would I do if it opened?

I wouldn't allow myself to entertain the notion that the Russians had won this battle. That was a slippery slope of possibilities. If they had, what happened to my family? My parents? My brother? What would happen to me? Would they kill me or worse? I didn't want to think about the possibilities that fell under the descriptive "worse." However, as a nineteen-year-old woman who'd lived her entire life within the Roríguez cartel, I knew the heinous crimes that occurred in the name of war.

My thoughts went to Emerald Club, a private club in Kansas City operated by the KC Mafia. My sister was married to the KC capo. When I visited her last summer, she took me inside the club. It wasn't during business hours, but I took in all that I could see. My family ran a similar private club in San Diego, Wanderland. While I've never been inside, I was aware of the array of businesses or services the club offered, just like at Emerald Club.

I'd listened to stories when the men thought they were unheard. My uncle Nicolas bragged about whores they'd acquired during a siege, whether Russian, Taiwanese, or Latinas from a rival cartel. Just because I was a virgin didn't mean I didn't know about sex. The thought turned my already-upset stomach. I'd rather be shot than made to work at a similar establishment for the Russian bratva. The chime of beeps from outside the sauna drew my attention away from my horrible thoughts to the door. I drew my knees closer to my chest, as if making myself smaller could save me from Russians if they were to enter.

Someone was trying to complete the combination in the secret room.

That meant the electricity was back on.

Miguel knew I wasn't in there.

Maybe it was Em looking for me.

That was the argument I used to calm my trembling.

I had the revelation that perhaps one of our people could be deceiving the intruders, telling them I was in the safe room. Maybe they gave them the wrong combination. The chimes began again, and then silence.

My hearing strained for a sound, any sound.

And then I heard it.

I willed my eyes to remain open as the door moved inward. A light from outside the room allowed me to see the lower legs and feet of the person entering. The sauna filled with light.

"Camila," my mother called as she crouched down, peering at me on the floor.

"Mama."

I scrambled from my hiding place. We collided before I could register her appearance. I pushed away and with my mouth agape, stared at her nightgown. The color of the material was hidden beneath the saturation of blood. A copper scent filled the air. It was then I noticed the stain on her hands.

Taking her sticky hand in mine, I asked, "Are you hurt?"

She pulled me back into her embrace and shook her head.

The door opened wider as Miguel and Em entered.

"You're safe," Em said.

"What...?" I tried to articulate a question.

My brother came closer. Under the bright lights I saw blood speckles on his face and shirt. The dark black cotton did a better job of hiding the crimson spray than on Mama's nightgown. He wrapped Mom and me in his arms. "Clean yourselves. You're leaving."

"Leaving, to where?" I asked.

"Papá's spoken to the capo dei capi."

"Dario." Our brother-in-law. It wasn't a question; I was simply trying to understand.

Mama reached for my shoulders. "We're going to Kansas City to Catalina."

"Is Papá okay?" I asked.

Em was the one to answer. "Three of the Russians are dead."

"Anyone of our people?"

Mama's eyes closed and her chin dropped. "Luis."

My heart ached as I shook my head. "No. Luis can't be dead."

"He saved me. The shot came from beyond the window." She shook her head. "I tried to save him."

The blood on her nightgown.

"Oh, Mama, I'm so sorry."

"If Miguel hadn't made me leave him, they probably would have gotten me too."

I turned to Miguel. "You saved us both."

"Doing my job."

Stepping away from my mother, I walked to Miguel and wrapped my arms around his torso. My vision blurred at the idea of losing him. I looked up. "Thank you."

Slowly, he wrapped his arms around me. "You're safe."

I didn't feel safe.

"Go to Kansas City," my brother said. "*El Patrón* has been notified. You two will be secure with Cat and the capo while we take out the Russian trash."

TWO

Camila

Miguel stayed omnipresent as I threw random clothes and belongings into a suitcase. Although the men had said we were safe, I couldn't help noticing the way my bodyguard was on ultra-high alert.

Tension caused my stomach to twist and goose bumps to dot my skin as we left my bedroom. Armed cartel guards stood outside my father's office door and still others could be seen over the banister down below in the foyer. From the hallway to my room, the roar of angry voices cursing in two languages came from Papá's office.

Moments before we reached the staircase, the office door flew open. My breath caught with surprise as

Dante, Dario Luciano's brother, appeared. His dark hair lay in waves. A gray t-shirt covered his wide chest. Muscles and tendons showed in his biceps. Instead of the suit he'd worn during Aléjandro's wedding, his long legs were covered by faded blue jeans. As incredible of a specimen he was to behold, it was his expression that held my attention and increased my unease.

A clenched jaw and pulsating muscles. His dark eyes bore into mine with an intensity I couldn't understand.

There was no questioning the rage in his countenance.

Appearing as surprised to see us as we were to see him, Dante stopped cold, his dark penetrating stare finally moving—scanning me from my head to my toes. I'd braided my long hair. My oversized sweatshirt hung to midthigh, and I'd changed from my sleeping shorts into a pair of exercise pants. Despite the fact the pants covered my legs to my ankles, by the way he was looking at me, I had the uncomfortable sensation that all my clothes had vanished.

His deep baritone voice sliced through the tension. "Are you hurt?"

Dante's question seemed foreign, his tone too soft to match his menacing glare. The incongruity between his tone and stare caused my lower stomach to twist. My ability to speak was out of reach as my pulse pounded as I took in the man before me.

Questions came without answers.

Dante wasn't a stranger, yet why was he in my house after the attack?

"No. She's safe," Miguel answered.

I nodded, leaning onto my bodyguard. "Why are you here?"

"I'm here to take you and your mother to Kansas City."

From everything I'd been told during my upbringing, I should be wary of the man who was now second-in-command in the Kansas City Famiglia. I should be frightened of the Mafia, but I wasn't. My sister married his brother. His sister married into the cartel. There was a bond that transcended the lifelong distrust, yet questions continued threatening my peace of mind from the fringe.

I peered up at Miguel. "I thought you were coming?"

He nodded. "*Sí.*"

Dante's lips curled. "Don't worry, little girl. Your father wouldn't allow you to travel with me if he had reason to question my intentions."

Little girl.

Asshole.

I stood taller and squared my shoulders. "Where's Mama?"

"Her room," Miguel answered.

"Tell her to hurry," Dante said.

Papá appeared in the frame of his office door. His dark gaze also scanned me, yet it felt fatherly, much different than Dante's intense stare. Papá lifted his arms. "Camila."

It was the first time I'd seen him since the invasion. I went forward, wrapping my arms around my father's torso. The warmth of his hug facilitated an unwanted release of emotions I'd kept at bay. Papá rubbed my back as tears dampened his shirt.

After a moment, he lifted my face. "You'll be safe, child." He tilted his chin toward Dante. "Mr. Luciano will take you and your *madre* to Catalina for a while."

I knew I didn't have a choice in the matter. Yet I had to question. "Why isn't the cartel transporting us?"

"Mr. Luciano was headed back today."

While I shouldn't be questioning, I couldn't seem to stop. My gaze went back and forth between Papá and Dante. "Why is he still here?"

Papá's forehead furrowed, no doubt growing weary of my insolence. "Mr. Luciano had business after Aléjandro's wedding."

I turned to Dante, wiping the tears from my cheeks. "What kind of business?"

An amused smile came to his full lips. "When you're older, you still won't be ready to hear the details."

His comments about my age were wearing on me. I stood taller. "I'm plenty old to understand death."

Before Dante could respond, Em appeared behind Papá. "Camila, hurry our *madre*. It's time for you both to go."

I had no idea what business Dante would have in San Diego, but by his answer, it was Mafia business. Could it have been against the cartel? If Dante was involved with the invasion, Papá wouldn't trust him with Mama and me. My mind was filled by a cyclone of disconnected thoughts. Maybe it made sense. Aléjandro's wedding was on Saturday. It didn't officially end until Sunday midday. Technically, this was only Monday.

"I'll check on Mama," I offered.

The men spoke quietly as I slipped down the hallway to my parents' wing. Without knocking, I opened the door to my parents' suite and scanned the large space. "Mama," I called out.

"In here," she replied, her voice coming from the bathroom.

Step by step, I approached the partially open door. I pushed it inward enough to see my mother dressed in slacks and a casual blouse. Her bloody nightgown from before was gone. Her long damp hair was pulled back in a low ponytail, indicating she'd taken the time to shower. My gaze went to her hands, the ones that only an hour ago were stained with blood. Her skin was pink from scrubbing, but the blood was gone. By the time I made my way back up to her eyes, I noticed how bloodshot and puffy they were.

"They want us to leave."

She nodded. "*Sì*, I'm almost ready."

Her voice was calm, almost too calm.

I went closer, inhaling the aroma of fresh bodywash, shampoo, and conditioner. It was a stark and welcome contrast to the harsh scent of blood and death. "Are you all right?"

She pressed her lips together and nodded. "We both will be. Your father will see to that."

"Did you know that Dario's brother, Dante, is still in California? We're going to Kansas City with him."

Her emerald eyes, the color of Catalina's and mine, opened wider. "I didn't know."

"Why would he still be here?"

"I don't know." She spoke as she gathered her cosmetics, placing them in a travel case.

I blurted out the question that had been creeping through my thoughts. "Can we trust the famiglia?"

Through the reflection in the mirror, Mama's stare came to mine. "We must. Think of Cat and their baby."

"But why didn't Dante go back to Kansas City with them? What if he had something to do with what happened?"

"You can't think that way." She let out a sigh. "If you spend your life questioning the men's motives or actions, you'll be consumed. We must trust them."

It wasn't exactly the answer I was looking for, yet it was an answer.

Out in their bedroom, Mama carried her cosmetics toward two large suitcases filled with clothes and shoes.

"You packed more than I did."

Her smile was weary. "If you ask me what I've packed, I won't be able to tell you. I only hope that it's enough and what I'll need."

I lifted my cheeks, trying to ease a bit of the tension. "Yeah, I don't know what I packed either. Whatever it was fit in one suitcase. I may have to raid Cat's closet."

"I'm sure she won't mind." Mama's eyes sparkled. "She would probably like you to. After all, her regular clothes are no longer fitting."

Yes, my sister was expecting her and Dario's first child in less than three months. The crowning jewel to the Mafia/cartel alliance. We both turned toward a knock on the door. Miguel stepped into the door frame.

"*Señora* Ruiz, may I help you with your luggage?"

Mama inhaled. "Thank you, Miguel."

My chest tightened at the knowledge that it would usually be Luis who helped Mama. That realization brought back the dreadful memories of what we'd endured. That terror was nothing compared to what happened to Luis. He was gone, giving his life for *mi madre*. "I'm ready to leave."

"This is our home, Camila. Don't let the Russians take that from you. If you do, you allow them to win."

I swallowed. "You're right. I'm...tired."

Mama wrapped her arm around my shoulders. "Of course you are. We can rest on the plane."

We were mostly quiet as Sergio drove the reinforced large SUV. From the third row of seats, I could see the back of everyone's heads. Dante rode in the front, next to Sergio. Mama and Miguel were in the middle row with me in the rear. Continually, my eyes went to Dante as if he had a magnetic force I couldn't fight.

If that were the case, it was a one-way fight. He hadn't said a word to me since making fun of my age. While almost twenty years old wasn't exactly aged, I wasn't a little girl either. I was an adult, one who had experienced a traumatic incident. The thought loosened a rogue tear to escape and slide down my cheek.

I turned and wiped the tear away with the back of my hand.

Crying wouldn't prove my point about my maturity.

Sergio drove the SUV around the airport to the area

25

that housed the private planes. He stopped in front of a white plane with 'Learjet' inscribed upon the tail. It wasn't marked with a name advertising that the plane belonged to the Luciano famiglia.

Mama and I followed Dante up the stairs as Miguel and Sergio secured our suitcases in the luggage hold. Mama stopped at the entrance, staring down the hull of the six-passenger jet.

"Dario and Catalina took the larger plane," Dante explained. "I wasn't expecting passengers, but we'll fit."

Mama looked at me and walked to the back of the plane. She took the last seat to the right, and I took the last one to the left. From the configuration, we'd have more privacy. The other four seats faced one another.

Dante remained standing, talking to the pilot and co-pilot. The co-pilot came back to our seats. "Mrs. Ruiz, Miss Ruiz, my name is Jeremy. We have limited supplies onboard; however, if you'd like anything to eat or drink, please don't hesitate to ask. I will do what I can."

"Thank you," Mama replied. "Water?"

"I'll have a bottle of water too," I said.

Jeremy smiled. "I can do that." He walked toward the front.

All the time Jeremy was talking and delivering our water, I couldn't help but notice the way Dante stood silently staring. There was something visceral in his dark gaze that I'd never before experienced.

Mama reached across the aisle and laid her hand on mine. "I'm so happy to spend time with Catalina, with both of my girls."

Nodding, I laid my head back against the soft leather.

If it made my mother feel better to think of this as a vacation, I wouldn't spoil her fantasy. Closing my eyes, I recalled the pool of blood—Luis's blood.

The water Jeremy delivered would need to wait. If I drank any now, I could end up in the lavatory, throwing it back up.

CHAPTER
THREE

Camila

W e'd been in the air for more than an hour, flying east toward the red hue radiating from the horizon. While my father and Dante Luciano had made quick work of getting Mama and I on the plane and away from the scene of the attack, my nerves remained in tatters. Every shift or bounce from turbulence had my knuckles blanching and my grip of the armrest tightening. Each time I closed my eyes, I remembered the opening of the sauna door and the dreadful seconds wondering if the Russians had found me. The horrible sights and smells lingered in my mind, from the shattered glass doors to the bloodstained tile. My childhood home had been violated in a way that

29

would stay with me long after the debris was cleaned away.

I turned to my side, taking in my mother as she sat staring out the small window. Neither of us had spoken much since the plane lifted off the ground. It was as if we both had too much to say yet neither was sure how to best verbalize our emotions.

"Are you all right?" I asked, not for the first time since our trauma.

She turned toward me, her expression stoic. Pressing her lips together, she shook her head. Tears teetered on her lower eyelids. As if held back by determination, they quickly faded away as she blinked, inhaled, and lifted her chin. "I don't want to scare you," she whispered to keep our discussion private.

"I'm not a child, Mama. I was there. I saw the blood and destruction. I don't think you can scare me any more than I was while I was hiding in the sauna."

"You should have been in the safe room."

"Miguel tried. With the power cut, the keypad wouldn't work."

"Your father will need to remedy that."

I didn't want to think about needing the room again.

Mom's nostrils flared as she took a ragged breath. "I've been trying to remember how long Luis had been with us."

I laid my hand over hers. "For about as long as I can remember."

She nodded. "I believe it was before Emiliano was born." She feigned a smile. "When your father and I were first married, he had a trusted bodyguard. His name was Alfonso."

"I don't recall that name."

"There was an ambush." She inhaled. "I think it was the first time I truly understood the danger in what your father does."

"Did something happen to Alfonso?" I asked.

"The two of them were out." Mom shook her head. "Andrés never shared all the details with me. I only knew they were both shot."

"Papá was shot?" How did I not know about this?

"It's not a story he approves of repeating. Alfonso was a good man. The bullet passed through him before striking Andrés. Your father walked away. Alfonso didn't. The shot came from another man Andrés thought he could trust."

"Someone in the Roríguez cartel?"

Mama sighed. "It was a very dangerous time. Your father and uncles were young. Your aunt Marie and I were young." Her lips curled into an almost smile. "Even Jorge was young, and Josefina, she was stunningly beautiful. I remember thinking that she could have been a model."

"Did she want that?"

"Her wants weren't relevant." Mama shook her head. "Her father was in charge. He never would have allowed her to have her own career. Josefina was his bargaining chip."

Lifting my eyebrows, my forehead furrowed. "Bargaining chip?"

"Juan Cruz didn't have a son. His daughter was his means to find the right person to peacefully take over his businesses."

"Josefina's father chose *el Patrón*?"

"It's the way of our world. Señor Cruz made a good choice. Jorge has done well." Her gaze went to the front of the plane.

Mine followed hers, wondering if Dante was listening. With earbuds in each ear and a laptop on the table in front of him, he seemed oblivious to our conversation.

"Did Josefina have any say in the matter?"

Mama turned to me. "Much like your sister."

I shook my head and let out a long breath.

She continued, "The Roríguez cartel wouldn't come into being for nearly another decade."

I wasn't sure why I hadn't thought more about the time when my parents were young. "Did you choose Papá?"

"Your grandfather did." She turned my way with wide eyes. "I was blessed. Andrés is a good man. I could have done much worse."

"Even in the Ruiz family," I said with a bit of snideness in my comment.

Mama's eyes narrowed. "We don't talk about family matters. You know that."

"Uncle Nicolas is good, but Uncle Gerardo—"

"Ximena," Mama interrupted, "was a good soul. Things will improve for Liliana."

Aunt Ximena passed away about a year ago, and while I never remember her being outwardly unhappy,

Uncle Gerardo's new wife, Liliana, is...well, turning into a shell of her former self. We're all worried.

I leaned back against the seat, seeing my mother in a whole new light. "How old were you when Papá was shot?"

Mama hummed as her eyelids fluttered. "I was seventeen when your father and I were married. This would have been about six months after that. I'd only recently learned I was pregnant."

"Seventeen," I repeated, "pregnant and the husband you barely knew was shot?"

"I was probably eighteen by then." She shook her head. "I was so scared. We had our whole lives to live, and our family hadn't even started. There was upheaval in the Cruz organization. This time..." She turned to me. "Last night was different. I've had my chance at life. All I could think about was you. I was so frightened for you, and then..."

"Luis?"

A rogue tear slid down Mama's cheek. "After Alfonso was killed, Andrés was very careful in who he hired to protect his family. When Luis came to us, he was a little older than your father. In all those years, he was always professional." Her smile returned. "And he loved you children." She tipped her chin toward the front of the plane. "As does Miguel."

I glanced up, seeing him staring in our direction.

"I'm so sorry about Luis."

"I didn't see Alfonso die. With all the death around us, until today, I've never seen it like that, where a strong and vital being is ripped from this world." She turned her hand and intertwined our fingers. "It's not something that anyone should see. I hope that you and Catalina can be spared that sight."

She didn't mention Em because he was born in the blood and death of the cartel. Seeing death was something Mama couldn't spare Em.

"You tried to save him." It wasn't a question. She'd told me, and I'd seen the blood.

"It was fruitless. I saw a red dot on his shirt. I keep thinking that if I would have said something, but I wasn't thinking straight. By the time I realized what it was, the shot rang out. He crumpled right next to me. I tried CPR." Her chin tipped down. "I was pushing. There was so much blood."

My stomach turned as I recalled the pool of blood near the broken glass doors. By the time they helped me from the sauna, Luis's body was gone. All the bodies were removed. Em said three Russians were also killed, yet I didn't see any of them.

"You did all you could," I reassured.

She lifted her face toward me. "I hope Luis knew how much he meant to our family."

Memories of Luis's service throughout my life came to mind. While Miguel was the one who spent the most time with us as children, Luis was often around. Like many men in the organization, he wasn't outwardly jovial. Catalina and I would try to make him laugh. We rarely succeeded, but we took a simple smile as a win. "I think he knew." I squeezed her hand. "And now we get to spend some time with Cat."

Mama nodded with a tired smile. "I'm grateful to Dario for allowing us to visit."

"I'm sure Cat had something to do with it."

"Camila, don't fool yourself into believing that our world is a place where you'll ever fully be allowed to make your own decisions."

The small hairs on the back of my neck stood to attention as I pulled my hand away. "Cat isn't in *our* world any longer."

Mama scoffed. "She will always be cartel." Her expression sobered. "I'm afraid that the world where she is now is darker. Her husband rules that world, *all* of it."

"What if I chose to not live in either world?"

She pressed her lips together. "After last night, I'm happy that you get to live."

Mama was right. I survived what I might not have survived. Leaning my head back against the soft leather seat, I made myself a promise. Whether it was a higher being, Miguel, my brother, others in the cartel, or all the above, I was alive. I wasn't going to waste my life living the way of my mother or sister. The last thing I wanted to do was live in a world without choices. I'd been given a second chance, and I would take it.

By the time we landed, we'd changed time zones, arriving in Kansas City midmorning.

A man named Giovanni waited with a car on the tarmac, ready to drive the four of us to Catalina's home. He greeted Dante as Miguel saw to our luggage.

Once again, Dante took the front passenger seat. This time, I sat between Miguel and Mama in the back seat.

Staring at the back of Dante's head, I thought about seeing him for the first time at Cat's wedding. Of course, I noticed him. I was paired with him—best man and maid of honor. If I were honest, during her wedding I was intimidated by both of the Luciano men—make that all of the Luciano Mafia men. They were tall, muscular, and undeniably handsome.

It wasn't until I visited Cat last summer that I was able to talk to Dario and Dante and get to know them in a less formal setting. I had no doubt that Cat and Dario would make their marriage work. The telltale signs were everywhere. During that visit, it was Dante who surprised me. By association, I knew he was a dangerous man; however, in reality, he was fun and talkative in a way that was the polar opposite of his older brother.

Before Aléjandro and Mia's wedding, I'd almost talked myself into asking Dante to dance. And then I saw him at the wedding. He was even more handsome than I'd remembered. Yet the fun man I'd met in Kansas City was gone. Dante's expression was dangerously beautiful and cold in a way that reminded me of his brother. While I watched him, I didn't think he noticed I was present. I could say the same about now.

He saw me as a child—a little girl. The way I felt around him wasn't love or even lust. It was probably the reemergence of the earlier intimidation. Surely, if I told my sister about my almost-crush on her brother-in-law, she'd probably tell me he was too old for me or worse, laugh.

My thoughts centered back to my sister as Giovanni pulled the car into an underground parking garage that I remembered from my last visit. I reached for my mother's hand. "We're almost there."

With the five of us and our luggage aboard the private elevator, we soared up to the top of the building, the penthouse. Dante, Giovanni, and Miguel took up more than their share of space as we stood facing the doors. As soon as they opened, I saw my sister.

"You're here," she said, practically bouncing as she opened her arms wide.

CHAPTER
FOUR

Dante

One deep breath was all it would take to bring my body in contact with Camila. My new favorite scent, that of cinnamon, was already invading my senses. While I'd done my best to keep my distance on the plane, now she was close enough that I could inhale her scent, sweet and cinnamon with the tempting aroma of innocence. Dario would say my thoughts were inappropriate. They were, and if I lingered in this position much longer, they would become even more inappropriate. The issue was that ever since I first heard of the invasion, I couldn't stop thinking about her. Camila was my first thought. Her safety. Her youth. Her beauty. Her standing within the cartel. I'd seen too many injustices in all my years on earth to not understand the horrible fate that could have awaited her.

My thoughts went back to hours earlier.

Throwing on a pair of blue jeans and t-shirt, I hurried to my rental car and sped through the dark San Diego streets until I reached the Ruizes' home. By the time I arrived, the grounds were swarming with cartel soldiers. It took a call from Andrés to convince the men at the gate to allow me entry. I gritted my teeth at the sight of the spilled blood on the pool deck and within their home.

The same fucking home where less than forty-eight hours ago, there had been a festive wedding. The Ruiz house staff was busy bleaching and cleaning away the evidence as I was taken upstairs to Andrés's home office.

When the door opened, I was met with a multitude of dark stares. After raising my hands, I pulled the revolver from my holster and made a show of laying it on Andrés's desk. The one rule my brother made clear when he called was not to do anything to upset the alliance.

By the palpable friction in the room, I wasn't feeling welcomed.

"I'm here to help."

Andrés appeared older than he had at Mia's wedding as he stood and offered me his hand. "Gracias."

"Tell me what the famiglia can do to help you."

The elevator doors opened to my sister-in-law. Valentina and Camila rushed forward. I didn't say a word, nodding to Catalina as I made my way toward Dario's office, the capo dei capi—boss of bosses—of the Kansas City Mafia.

Dario had that title for almost a year. Upon our father's death, he'd taken the position he'd been born to hold.

Change wasn't easy under any circumstances; however, our father's indecisiveness preceding his death didn't facilitate an easy transfer of power. Father had said he would step down as capo as soon as Dario wed. He didn't.

A bullet from Alesia Moretti, father's mistress, accelerated Dario's rise to power. Our father was no longer our concern. Currently and permanently, Vincent Luciano would preside over the devil's angels, quite possibly vying for the top job against Satan himself.

As with such a transition, there were members of the outfit who weren't pleased that Dario assumed the role he'd been promised. At the time of our father's demise, my brother was only thirty-six years old. Many with more wrinkles and gray hair thought the position should have gone to one of our father's brothers.

Dario and I worked tirelessly to create a cohesive outfit. Tolerance for disloyalty was nonexistent. The former soldiers, capos, and associates would work with Dario Luciano, or their terms of service would be permanently severed.

The first few months were the most difficult.

Neither Dario nor I wanted to end the lives of people who had been loyal to our father. Then again, you know what they say about one rotten apple. Now, nearly a year later, the purge was complete. That didn't mean it wasn't a constant job to ensure continued fidelity.

The rather recent alliance between the Luciano famiglia and the Roríguez cartel proved to be a double-edged sword. Or in our world, a sharp fucking knife. To

41

say that Dario was committed to the alliance was like saying that winter was cold, or summer was hot.

Last June, Dario wed Catalina Ruiz, the elder daughter of a Roríguez cartel lieutenant. In another few months, the alliance will further be solidified with the birth of their first child. If anyone had a problem with the famiglia and cartel unification, they had a problem with their boss. Fucking with the alliance wasn't something Dario would allow.

That was why I was now entering my brother's office. In our newly redefined organization, I was now my brother's underboss and his consigliere. It was in that capacity that I stayed in San Diego after our sister's wedding. There were a few business deals I wanted to see for myself.

Dario looked up from behind his desk, his dark stare meeting mine. Newfound tension radiated from his being, emanating from his pores, and displayed in the taut muscles and tendons in his neck and jaw. "What the fuck do you know?" he asked as I entered.

Shutting the door, I walked closer. "Not a lot more than you. Catalina's family was attacked—their home."

Her parents.

Her brother.

Her sister.

My mind inappropriately went back to Camila. Her petite figure, delicate fingers, large green eyes, the way her maid-of-honor dress hugged her curves. I even had visions of her at Mia's wedding. I'd kept my distance, but that didn't mean I hadn't noticed how nicely she'd grown up in the last year. And then seeing her this morning outside her father's office—it took all my self-control not to reach for her and to assess that she wasn't harmed.

I wanted to strip off that sweatshirt and verify her lack of injuries.

Dario stood. "One of their guards was killed. What did you learn about anyone else? Getting fucking information from our new brother-in-law is slow and tedious."

The capo dei capi was wearing his usual formal attire. His custom suit coat hung from the back of his chair. His button-down white shirt was crisply starched, and diamond cuff links glistened at his wrists. Besides the physical clues, the only outward sign of his stress was that his normally perfectly styled dark hair was tousled as if he'd run his hands through it more than once.

I continued my report, "Aléjandro was on his way from the Bella, Jorge's floating mansion, when I left with the women. According to Andrés, Mia is out there too."

Dario exhaled. "How are Valentina and Camila?"

"Scared but unharmed," I replied.

Dario nodded. "I'd told Andrés to send them here. Your still being in San Diego was fortunate."

"I did what we talked about yesterday, getting a feel for their operation. I was going to go to visit a few other cartel drop-offs today." I shrugged. "Instead, I got to babysit the women."

"They're Catalina's fucking mother and sister."

Shit. I wasn't complaining. My brother was definitely wound tight. "What does Catalina know?"

"The basics. She was asleep when I got the call. With traveling to and from California for Mia's wedding, she's worn out. I waited until she woke."

I settled in one of the seats across from Dario's desk. "I didn't stop to talk to her." I needed to make space between Camila and me. "How did she take it?"

"Not well." His nostrils flared. "She was better when she learned Valentina and Camila would be coming here."

Dario stood and gripped the back of his tall leather chair and pressed his lips together before adding, "There's more."

Leaning forward, I stared at my brother. "What?"

"Last night, earlier in the evening, Mia and Aléjandro's new home was ransacked. No one was hurt. Apparently, no one was there."

"The fuck? Why wasn't I told." I thought of something he said. "No one was at their home?"

"Aléjandro had guards outside, but he believes the perpetrators came from the ocean, unseen by the guards. It's a situation he decreed to resolve."

"Fuck," I sighed as I leaned back. "That wasn't mentioned when I was at the Ruizes' home. Two separate incidents seem unlikely."

Dario nodded. "No one was aware you stayed in California. I had to convince them you weren't part of the invasion."

They thought I might be involved. "No wonder they all sent death stares as I entered Andrés's office."

Dario walked to the highboy and filled his coffee cup.

Turning to me, he lifted his eyebrows in a silent question, regarding coffee.

"No, I already drank a pot. As for the invaders, the cartel killed three of the Russians. There was a fourth one. They took him to the basement at Wanderland for questioning." My lips curled. "I would have been happy to stay in San Diego and help with the interrogation."

Dario's millisecond of an expression change was the first hint that his face hadn't turned to stone. Even his voice was a tad lighter. "Did you offer?"

"I did. They turned me down."

"From what I've been told, our new brother-in-law excels at the same thing."

"Yeah, but if I were there, we could cut off appendages twice as fast. It could be brotherly bonding."

Dario shook his head. "Your suggestion wasn't the only one turned down. I offered to send some of our men."

Lifting my eyebrows, I asked, "Andrés turned you down?"

"It's not Andrés's call. It's Aléjandro's. I even had a short conversation with Jorge. He's not happy, but thank God they caught the Russians." Dario's shoulders relaxed. "*El Patrón* told me the same thing about the Bella. Mia is safe on his boat."

"I heard it's secret and strategic."

"It is," Dario replied. "The boat is a fucking superyacht, like something oligarchs own. When *el Patrón* is on the yacht flying the Mexican flag in international waters, he isn't subject to US laws."

"So, our sister is floating someplace...what twenty-five to thirty miles off the coast of California?"

"Roughly." Dario paced behind his desk. "Aléjandro turned down our men, said they had to deal with it their way."

"Probably better."

"Why?"

"Mia and Aléjandro's house. Catalina's family. Aren't you seeing the connection?"

"Yes, I'm seeing it. That's why we should have men out there. Mia is still a Luciano."

A smirk came to my lips. "Just like Catalina is still a Ruiz."

"No." He sent daggers from his stare. "Yes. Fuck you. I want to do something. They're suffering because of our alliance."

"You're doing something. You've taken in Catalina's sister and mother." I looked around the stately office. "If this place had been attacked, wouldn't you feel better if your wife was somewhere where you knew she was protected?"

"Allies...fucking family were attacked. I don't want to babysit my mother-in-law and a child."

"Camila isn't a child. She's the same age as Jasmine."

"Oh, right, they're fucking adults."

"By definition."

Dario's jaw tensed. "I don't want definitions. I want to track down whoever is behind this."

"You want blood."

He nodded. "I want fucking blood."

"I would assume that's the same thing Jorge and

Aléjandro want. Our new brother-in-law isn't second-in-command because of his annoying personality or because he's a pompous ass who won't accept help. He'll get the job done." I stood. "Listen, when the negotiations started for Mia's hand, I wasn't sure..." I lifted my hand to stop Dario's rebuttal. "...I mean, I kind of kicked his ass at your wedding. But as we learned more about him, I became convinced. Mia's safe on some multimillion-dollar yacht, and the two Ruiz ladies will be here. That gives Aléjandro and the rest of the cartel the peace of mind to get their job done."

"We need to up our manpower on the street. Depending on who's pulling the Russians' strings or financing their operation, they could bring it here to Kansas City. I'm sure as hell not putting my wife in their crosshairs."

"Or her mother and sister," I added.

"They'll all stay put for the time being. I know you've already been awake a fucking day. So have I. Right now, I need you to hit the streets and get word out to the capos. I want everyone in the famiglia to be on the lookout for something coming from the Russians. Out west it was probably either Kozlov's or Volkov's organization. If it was either one of them, then they could easily be in contact with Myshkin in St. Louis or Ivanov in Detroit."

"You think Myshkin would seek help from the Detroit bratva?"

Myshkin.

The name made the small hairs on my arms stand to attention.

"We have to be on the lookout for anything."

47

I agreed. "We need to take that bratva scum down once and for all."

"Get yourself cleaned up. This information needs to come from the top, and you're the top next to me. Make everyone understand that we're talking code-red importance."

I looked down at my clothing. "I'm clean enough for the streets." I didn't wait for Dario's response. He was the boss in the suit. I was the man who got shit done while blending in and standing above. "Do you want me to tell them what happened in San Diego?"

Dario inhaled. "Yes. Tell them what they need to hear, not where anyone is staying. Only tell them that the second-in-command and a top lieutenant of the Roríguez cartel both had their homes invaded. If our people get the truth from us, they won't believe the lies Myshkin's men spread on the streets."

"Will do." I tilted my head. "What is your next move?"

"Welcome my in-laws for an indeterminate-length-of-time visit. Oh, and let them know that for the time being, they're grounded."

I scoffed. "I'd rather be on the streets."

"Me too."

FIVE

Camila
A little earlier

I tried not to notice Dante hurrying past us without a word. My concentration was on my sister. Even though we'd recently seen her at the wedding, I couldn't get over how she absolutely glowed, dressed like a stereotypical Mafia wife in a flowing white pantsuit, large chunky gold jewelry, and low heels. Her long dark hair spilled over her shoulders in waves. Leaving our luggage behind, Mama and I rushed toward Catalina. The opulent surroundings were a blur. This wasn't my first visit to Dario and Catalina's home, and in my opinion, the opulent surroundings weren't as stunning as my sister. We both stepped back, peering down at Cat's growing midsection.

"How are you feeling?" Mama asked.

"Tired," Cat said with a smile. "We only returned from California yesterday." She reached for each of our hands and squeezed as tears teetered on her eyelids. "How are you both?"

"Glad we're here," I said.

"I couldn't believe it when Dario told me." My sister laid her hand over her round belly as her gaze went to Miguel. After tilting her head, she went to him and wrapped her arms around his torso.

"Mrs. Luciano."

Stepping back, she shook her head. "I'm still Catalina." Her smile grew. "Thank you for keeping them safe."

Miguel nodded.

Contessa, Cat's housekeeper, appeared. "Welcome." After our greetings she directed the two men to take our luggage to our assigned bedrooms.

As the three of us made our way into Cat's living room, my sister pressed against her stomach as her expression contorted. "Our little one has been very active."

Biting my lip, I watched as Mama laid her hand over Cat's stomach. It didn't take long for Mama's sad expression from earlier to disappear as she felt her first grandchild move and kick.

"Do you want to feel?" Cat asked, looking at me.

"I mean, if you don't mind."

Cat reached for my hand. "Don't be afraid to push. I promise I won't break."

It took a few seconds, but then I too had a large smile. "Oh my God. There's a baby in there."

Catalina laughed. "I sure hope so." Sunlight streamed

through the floor-to-ceiling windows, creating an aura around her as she sat near the end of a sofa. "Tell me, are you both all right?"

Mama and I took seats, me in a nearby chair and Mama next to Catalina. Over the course of the next thirty or more minutes, we both recounted what we knew and remembered of the nighttime ambush.

"Dario hasn't said much," Cat said, "but I heard him talking on his phone to Dante. I'm so glad he was still in California to bring the two of you here."

"Why was he still there?" I asked.

"Camila," Mama chastised.

"It's a simple question. He must have planned to stay longer than you and Dario. I mean, he had a plane waiting."

Cat shrugged. "I don't know."

My nose scrunched. "I thought Dario talked to you."

"He does," Cat replied defensively. "Dante flew into San Diego after us. In all honesty, I was too concerned that traveling wouldn't be good for the baby to have been thinking about anyone else."

"You just entered your third trimester," Mama said. "You're a healthy young woman. You shouldn't worry. Normal activities are safe."

A pink hue filled my sister's cheeks as she looked down and back up, inhaling. "I'm sure Papá would have supplied you with a plane. This just worked out easier."

"Almost too easy," I muttered under my breath.

Mama shot a look in my direction. "Andrés didn't mean for me to overhear, but yesterday evening, Aléjandro and Mia's new home was ransacked."

"What?" Cat and I asked together.

"Was Mia hurt?" Cat asked with genuine concern.

Mama shook her head. "No one was home. The break-in was why the two of them went out on the Bella."

Catalina's green eyes opened wide. "Mia's on the Bella. Oh, wait until I tell Dario."

"I didn't know about their house," I said, "but the Bella would be a great honeymoon if it wasn't with Aléjandro."

Catalina laughed before asking, "Was Rei at your house during the attack?"

Mama shook her head. "What I overheard was that Jorge wanted both the boys on the Bella."

Boys. Aléjandro and Rei were both older than me.

I stood. "See, this is suspicious. If *el Patrón* knew there was danger and then we were attacked..."

Cat questioned, "Could the two invasions be connected?"

Mama inhaled. "There's a common denominator."

"The famiglia," Cat said, covering her pregnant belly, her expression sobering. "You could have been hurt because of me."

"No," Mama protested. "You did what was expected of you, just as I'm sure Mia did. The alliance isn't the problem. The problem is other people's opinion about the alliance."

"Other people?" I asked. "Cartel or famiglia?"

Cat shook her head. "It could be either or both. Dario's been communicating with *el Patrón*." She met

Mama's gaze. "I'm so sorry about Luis. He was a good man."

"He was."

Catalina stood. "No more talk of attacks or deaths. I'm so happy to have the two of you here for a while. And I bet you're both tired. Let's go in the kitchen and see what Contessa has planned for lunch and then, if you want, you can rest."

"Or we could get out of here." I flashed my sister a smile. "I know, we could take Mom to Emerald Club."

Cat closed her eyes and shook her head. "Camila, you're obsessed."

"Well, you know, I was almost kidnapped by the bratva. It got me thinking about the sex workers." When Mama looked at me, aghast, I continued, "You know, if I was forced to become one."

"Stop," Mama commanded. "No more talk of such things. You're both ladies. Just because things like that exist, we don't need to discuss it."

It wasn't Mama's words, but my sister's pleading look that made me change the subject. Looking around, I took in the lovely surroundings. "Is Jasmine here?"

Jasmine was...it was a long story, but she grew up with Cat's husband, Dario. Cat thinks of her as his daughter even though they aren't related by blood or marriage. Yes, it's complicated.

"She's back in New York," Cat said. "She found a part-time job at a museum near the university."

"A museum?" Mama asked. "What's her major?"

"She has a double major," Cat replied with pride.

"She's studying history, particularly the Renaissance, and archaeology."

"Wow," I said, thinking about my major of interior design.

Cat went on, "Dario has always been a collector of fine things and unbeknownst to him, his interest sparked hers."

Mama's smile grew. "Cat, there's so much more to your husband than we were told."

"There is," Cat agreed. "In a world of danger, he's a good man."

Mama looped her arm with Cat's. "I'm proud of you." She turned to me. "And of you too."

I lifted my hands. "I'll let Cat be married and have the babies. I want to see more of the world than SoCal and Missouri."

"Is there more?" Cat asked with a grin.

Our conversations around the kitchen quieted as Dario entered. I couldn't help but think that it must be difficult to live with a man who exuded power the way the capo dei capi did. It surrounded him like an impenetrable cloud. Without uttering a word, he'd garnered all our attention.

"Valentina," he said in a deep, pleasing voice, going to Mama and offering her an embrace.

Catalina's smile shone, lighting up the room.

"Dario," Mama said, "thank you for opening your home to Camila and me."

"This is Catalina's home too." He almost grinned. "And you're always welcome."

"Camila."

The mention of my name drew my attention back to my brother-in-law. I'd mindlessly been watching the swing door, hoping that Dante would follow. My gaze met Dario's. "Thank you."

He cleared his throat. "I don't know how to put this another way." He had our attention. "Until we can be certain of what's happening, I'd like the three of you to remain in the apartment."

Pressing my lips together, I looked from my mother to my sister. They were both nodding obediently. "Are we talking hours, days, weeks?" I asked.

"Camila," Mama chastised.

The swinging door opened as Dante stepped in. His dark eyes searched our faces before settling back on Dario. "Oh, this is the 'you are forbidden to go anywhere' speech, isn't it?" Before Dario or anyone could respond, Dante went on, his lips curling into a grin, "Who was asking about how long?"

"That was me," I said bravely, taking in the definition in his muscular arms.

His brown-eyed gaze came to me, warming my circulation. "I'm sure you can find something to keep you busy while we make sure that Kansas City is safe."

"It's not a problem," Mama replied, reaching for my hand. "Is it, Camila?"

"I'd rather go to Emerald Club, but I suppose hanging out here is almost as exciting."

Dante's smile twitched, before he turned to Dario, asking to speak to him alone.

After lunch, I slipped away, going upstairs to the same room where I'd stayed on my last visit. On the big bed, I found my suitcase. While it was only early afternoon in Kansas City, Mama and I had been awake since the alarms rang over eight hours ago. I opened my suitcase and found a pair of shorts and a t-shirt before stripping out of my travel clothes.

The warm water of the shower sprayed over my skin as the emotions of the long day bubbled out of me. Tears I'd held back since Papá's hug streamed down my cheeks as sobs came from my chest. It was the first time since the attack that I truly allowed myself to recognize the trauma. The scents of shampoo, conditioner, and body-wash filled the humidity with sweetness. With my stomach full and my body washed, I chose to climb under the covers in the large bed.

Sleep came quickly, whisking me into dreamland.

At the raging of the alarms, I woke to the sound of screaming. It took me a moment to realize that I was the one yelling. Clamping my lips together, I quickly sat up, scooted against the headboard, and with trembling hands, pulled the blankets up to my shoulders. Peering around the bedroom, I saw everything, from my suitcase and clothes strewn about to the solid furniture. I hadn't closed the blinds. The sky beyond the window was light blue with fluffy white clouds.

There was absolutely no reason for me to have screamed.

No alarms.

No intruders.

No need for a safe room.

Did Catalina have a safe room? Did I want to know that answer?

Closing my eyes, I thought back to the invasion. I couldn't remember screaming or even crying while it was happening. If I didn't scream then, why was I doing it now?

I checked my phone and learned it was after five in the afternoon.

In the bathroom, I splashed my face with cool water and stared into my green eyes. My hair in my reflection was a mess. My choice was to wet my hair down again or braid the wavy tangles into submission. I chose the braid. As I looked through my clothes for something appropriate to wear to dinner, I remembered Dante's dinnertime visits when I was last here.

There wasn't any rhyme or reason to the clothes I packed. Maybe my sister wouldn't mind if I borrowed a sundress. I'd also add a little makeup and a dab of perfume. Dante may not notice me, but if he did, I wanted him to see I wasn't a little girl.

I stopped walking outside Catalina's suite at the sound of voices within.

She used to tell me that I was the master eavesdropper. I wasn't really. It was more opportunistic. Quietly, I leaned closer to the door.

CHAPTER
SIX

Camila

Closing my eyes, I concentrated on Cat and Dario's conversation.

"How long do you plan to keep us under lock and key?"

"This isn't a prison sentence. Things have been..." His voice trailed off.

"I understand. It's that while Mama won't complain; Camila—"

My skin bristled at the mention of my name.

"I don't know how long," Dario interrupted. "My number one concern is that you're safe—they're safe. You and your family are the center of this alliance."

"The alliance," Catalina replied, "is with *el Patrón,* not my family."

"We're all involved."

"You don't need to worry about Mia out on the Bella." My sister's voice softened. "She's safe."

"I'm not worried about Mia; I'm worried about the alliance." Dario's volume increased. "I'm worried about you. The Russians attacked two targets, two targets in San Diego with an affiliation with this famiglia. It's a rational concern to worry that they will try to attack here."

"What about Jasmine?"

Dario's tone changed, sounding even more protective. "I've sent Armando to New York."

Catalina's response was inaudible.

Dario continued, "He's going to assess Piero's work. I trust Armando, especially when it comes to Jasmine. If he thinks she's in danger, he'll bring her home." Dario scoffed. "Don't worry. Contessa is thrilled to have a full house to care for."

"I'm sure she didn't bargain for my family."

"You're *my* family, Catalina. Your family is my family. It's why I offered Aléjandro some of our soldiers."

"You did?" There was noticeable surprise in her voice.

"I did. He turned me down, but I offered. I have a meeting in a few minutes down in my office. It would be best if your mother and sister..."

Catalina sighed. "They're both resting. Will the meeting be over before dinner?"

"I'll do my best."

"I'll stay up here."

My skin grew uncomfortably tight as the voices dimmed and low moans came from the other side of the door. As Dario said his goodbye, I hurried down the hallway away from their room and slipped inside the first door.

It didn't take me long to realize I was in Jasmine's bedroom. I scanned the colorful comforter and pillows. Within the built-in bookcases were books and pictures. Curiously, I chewed on my lower lip as I went closer. She had pictures with friends. I suddenly wondered how different it was to grow up in the Mafia than it was in the cartel.

One picture caught my eye.

It was Jasmine with a woman I didn't know. She was pretty and petite. In a way she resembled Jasmine, but she was older with dark hair versus Jasmine's red hair. Catalina had told me the story of Jasmine's sister and Dario. This must be a picture of the infamous Josie.

Footsteps in the hallway alerted me when Dario left his room. I waited a minute or two before opening the door to the hallway and peering in both directions. Letting out a breath, I stepped out, closed Jasmine's door, and walked to Catalina's door. With a rap of my knuckles, I knocked.

"Come in," Catalina called.

Opening her door, I stepped inside.

"Oh, Camila. I didn't realize you were done resting."

I looked down at the shorts and t-shirt I'd put on after my shower. "I wasn't exactly thinking straight when I packed to come here." I tilted my head with a grin. "You wouldn't have any dinner-appropriate casual dresses I could borrow, would you?"

My sister's smile grew. "Just like old times." She

stood from the sofa where she'd been sitting and gestured for me to follow to her closet.

The room, because it was too big to describe as a closet, was filled with exquisite items, from dresses to tops, blouses, skirts, and slacks. Multiple sets of drawers lined the walls and in the center of the room was a large round ottoman. "I'll just take your entire closet."

Catalina laughed. "Let me find my nonmaternity clothes. You can borrow as many as you'd like." She laid her hand over her baby bump. "Obviously, they won't fit me."

"Any word on what's happening on the streets?" I asked.

My sister shook her head as her smile faded. "I'm sorry we can't go shopping or out and about in the city. Dario is protective."

Overprotective.

"I get it." I began pushing hangers from side to side, checking out Catalina's clothes racks. "Papá would probably do the same thing." I craned my neck, looking at my sister over my shoulder. "You know, keeping us safe is their way of controlling us."

"Maybe. Remember Occam's razor?"

I rolled my eyes. "Are we back in psychology class?"

"What does it say?"

"The simplest explanation is usually the one closest to the truth."

Catalina nodded. "So, when Dario says he wants to keep us safe, he means...?" She left the sentence open.

"He wants to keep us safe."

My sister grinned. "Are you finding anything you want to borrow?"

To avoid daily trips to my sister's closet, I chose four sundresses, a nicer dress, and a couple of tops. Once back in my room, I changed into an emerald-green and blue dress, pairing it with sandals with straps that wound around my ankles. The neckline wasn't too low for Mama to comment on, but when I looked in the mirror, I liked the way it made the top of my breasts noticeable.

My prepping was in vain—not only wasn't Dante at dinner, but neither was Dario.

With each passing day, I felt more and more trapped within the walls of Catalina's home. I'd spend my time in my room on my laptop or phone or in the theater room. I even ventured into the library from time to time.

The only thing that kept me from going stir-crazy was my new obsession with Dante. I'd wander the lower level of the penthouse simultaneously hoping to find him while nervous of what I'd say if I did. The few times he joined us for dinner, he was a mix of personalities. The jovial man I'd met a year ago was a bit darker, more intense.

That personality was equally interesting and even a bit more intriguing.

Five days into our visit, I sat at dinner, pushing Contessa's meal around my plate. It was hard to be hungry when I felt like I wasn't doing anything to create an appetite. The conversation around me wasn't registering until I heard the shift in Dario's tone.

"We should discuss that in private."

It was a warning I'd heard my father say to my

brother on more than one occasion. I looked around the table, wondering what exactly I'd missed. Dante's muscles tightened beneath his Dri-FIT short-sleeve shirt. There was a sharp edge to his jaw as he stabbed the roasted lamb on his plate. Mama and Catalina were eating quietly.

It was Dario's gaze that met mine. "That isn't a discussion you should have to hear." His tone was lighter than a moment before.

"I didn't," I replied honestly. "But if I had been paying attention, that would have been all right too. I grew up in the same home as Cat. I haven't exactly been sheltered from the ways of the cartel."

"Camila," Mama whispered.

Dario nodded with a slight grin. However, it was Dante's stare that I felt scorching my skin. My flesh pebbled as I turned to him. Lifting my chin, I sat taller. "I'm not a little girl." I hadn't refuted his comment when he made it nearly a week ago. Obviously, it had been eating at me.

Dario lifted his eyebrows. "Do you know who says they're not a little girl?"

I laid my fork beside my plate. "Anyone who isn't a little girl."

"On the contrary. The need to announce who you are or who you're not serves the exact opposite purpose." He inhaled, his nostrils flaring. "Nevertheless, our dinner conversation will remain appropriate for everyone present."

The capo had spoken. Despite the way the small hairs on the back of my neck stood to attention, I knew better than to continue the conversation. Catalina once explained that Jasmine and I were the same age. It made sense that Dario would see me as a child. I peered up, lifting my eyes as my face looked down at my plate. Dario wasn't my concern. It was the man with the smirk across the table.

CHAPTER
SEVEN

Dante

My apartment was one floor, as opposed to Dario's two. Nevertheless, the four-bedroom floorplan was more than enough space for a single man. With access to the capo dei capi's home, I wasn't exactly bringing women to my bedroom. Other than Contessa's once-a-week visit to clean—keeping things from getting too out of hand—rarely did anyone come by. If Dario wanted me, he'd call me to him.

Wearing nylon basketball shorts and a t-shirt, I had my heart set on getting some sleep. More than likely, I'd be called out to the Kansas City streets. As I sat at my kitchen counter with my tablet, reading the day's reports from the capos on the street, the unexpected sound of the elevator stopping caught my attention, making my ears buzz.

A brief glance out the large windows confirmed what I already knew. It was late, too late for Contessa, or on the rare occasion, Dario, to make an unannounced visit. I assured myself that the bratva wouldn't be brazen enough to enter my apartment. Then again, they'd invaded the Ruiz home.

Calmly, I removed my gun from my holster and silently moved to a vantage point with visibility to the elevator. With my finger on the trigger, arms locked, and sight set on the opening doors, I was prepared to kill the intruder.

"Fuck," I murmured as Camila stepped from the elevator and into my sights. I lowered my gun. "Little girl, you were almost shot." I set the safety and returned it to my holster.

A nervous smile curled her lips as a pink hue climbed from her neck to her cheeks.

Still wearing the long green dress from tonight's dinner, Camila was absolutely stunning. Thin spaghetti straps draped over her slender shoulders and the material tightened around her breasts and trim waist. The neckline gave me just a peek at her small breasts she hid beneath the fabric. Her long dark hair cascaded down her back.

I'd tried to avoid staring during dinner. Now that she was standing in my living room, I couldn't look away. I shook my head. "Does your sister or mother know where you are?"

Camila tugged on her pink bottom lip with her teeth as the emerald of her eyes stared up at me. "No. I'm claustrophobic in that apartment. This is the only place I can go."

"You shouldn't be able to get here."

She smiled, lifting a small card with a sensor. "I borrowed this."

In two strides I was to her, taking the card from her hand. Her cinnamon scent was like Viagra to my dick. I tried to stay focused. "Who let you borrow this?"

"Hey," she protested. "I need that to get back upstairs."

I slipped the card into the pocket of my basketball shorts. "Who let you borrow their card?" I asked louder than before.

"No one." She dipped her chin. "I stole it from Contessa."

"You *stole* it?"

"Oh, come on. Like you've never committed crimes."

Murder.

Theft.

Bodily injury.

Disposing of bodies.

Blackmail.

Fraud.

The list went on.

Admittedly, in the right company, it was an impressive record.

"Crimes are what I do. You, on the other hand, are a—"

"Do not say *little girl*." Camila took a step toward me, bringing her close, too close. Laying her hands on my chest, she leaned closer, pushed up on her toes and brought her lips to mine.

The hell?

No, heaven.

My body and mind warred as I kissed her back, bringing my hands to her hips and pulling her closer. I'd been intimate with many women, yet there was something about this pint-sized woman that sent sparks and flickers through my bloodstream. Camila tasted like sweetness and sunshine—forbidden fruit. My mind caught up as I pushed her away, my stare drilling into hers. "Are you trying to get me killed?"

She shook her head. "No, never. I wanted to show you that I'm not a child. I'm a woman."

I felt my cheek rise with a lopsided grin. "And what would your father say if he knew we kissed?"

Her eyes sparkled. "My father doesn't need to know." When I didn't respond, she continued, "Or my mother or Cat. I've never been kissed before. I wanted it to be with you."

"You still haven't been kissed." Dario would fuck me over if he knew what I was contemplating.

"Yes, we just—"

Slowly, I shook my head, my gaze locked on her stunning stare. I took a step closer, heat building around us as electricity snapped and crackled with the warning of an impending storm. Camila Ruiz was too young, too delicate, and too pure for a man like me. The Mafia and cartel had two marriages securing our alliance.

Spoiling a cartel princess could ruin everything.

I shut my mind down in considering right versus

wrong. After all, I wasn't a man who was guided by such simplistic standards. A few days ago, my knife was covered in another man's blood. His body was now dissolving in a vat of acid.

Dante Luciano was as far from a choirboy as they could come.

Yet, there was something more primal at work, maybe even something I could justify as altruistic.

Camila wanted to be kissed.

Another step.

Camila's eyes grew impossibly larger, and her lips opened slightly as she backed away from me. Our feet moved in sync, one and then the other. Her breathing came faster, causing her breasts to push against her dress. The material tented over beaded nipples.

"You still haven't been kissed," I repeated, my tone lower and my words slower. "You've kissed."

She inhaled as she came to a stop, her shoulders colliding with the wall. She straightened her neck and squared her shoulders as if she wasn't trapped by a man double her weight with a growing hard-on.

Her voice was strong with determination. "I'm almost twenty years old. I want to decide who kisses me, not my father and not *el Patrón*."

My pulse raced as I laid my forearm on the wall above her head. "Have you been promised to another?"

She shook her head. "Not that I've been told. It's just watching Cat with Dario...I want to make my own choice." Camila lifted her gaze, keeping her eyes on me.

The heat of her small body radiated through my cotton shirt, stimulating every nerve ending and rerouting my circulation. There would be no hiding my hardening cock in the damn shorts. "Are you sure you want to be kissed?"

She swallowed and nodded.

Reaching for her chin, I gently angled her face to the perfect position.

Her wide eyes watched as I leaned over her, bringing my lips back to hers. My hand slid around to her neck, fisting her long hair.

Unlike her first attempt, this kiss came with a combination of force and restraint. Her soft lips pushed back against mine. I fought the compulsion to slip my tongue into her warm haven.

Camila's hands slid up to my shoulders and higher, her fingers weaving through my hair. I closed the gap between us, pressing my erection against her stomach before giving into my desire and sliding my tongue between her lips.

Her moans encouraged me to continue.

This was wrong and felt so right.

With the tension surrounding our father's death and Dario's takeover, our constant battles with the bratva, the fight in San Diego, and the trauma of the Ruiz invasion, this—right here—was the first moment in as long as I could remember that made my heart race and set off synapses throughout my nervous system. It was as if the stars aligned, bringing the two of us together in the right place at the right time.

Releasing Camila's hair, I bunched the skirt of her dress higher until I grasped her thigh and wrapped it around my hip. Camila gasped as I leaned in, pressing my hardness against her core. Pulling away from our kiss, I searched her expression for an indication I'd gone too far.

"Have you had enough of your first kiss?"

She shook her head. "No, I like it."

Definitely not a little girl.

I ran the pad of my thumb over her swollen lips. "You like it?" I asked with a grin.

Camila nodded. "I'm afraid this isn't real, and I'll wake up."

I knew how she felt. If this was a dream, I didn't want it to fucking end.

Lowering my face, I brought our lips back together. The ferocity was still there, but I slowed, savoring her sweetness as my hips ground against her. Soon she was pressing back, bouncing to my rhythm. Her breaths came quicker as whimpers filled my ears.

I imagined pushing her panties to the side and slipping a finger or two into her virgin core. My thoughts swelled in proportion to my cock as I fantasized about how tight she would be. I was a grown-ass man dry-humping like a fucking teenager, and it could possibly be the best sex I'd ever had.

"Oh," she called out, her fingernails digging into my shoulders.

"That's it, ride it out, beautiful."

Camila pressed her core against my hardness.

I watched in awe as her eyes closed and her lips parted. Watching her climax was intoxicating. It was a vision I would never tire of seeing. Finally, she dropped her forehead to my shoulder. I released her thigh, giving her two feet on the floor to keep her balance. Still, I held her close until her breathing evened.

When she lifted her face and our eyes met, I smiled. "Has anyone ever made you come before?"

She hesitated for only a moment before answering, "No."

"A night of firsts."

Her cheeks pinkened. "Should I be embarrassed?"

I shook my head. "You're gorgeous, Camila. Being you, making your wants and needs known...it's sexy as fuck." I ran my thumb over her swollen lips. "If anyone sees you, they'll know you've been kissed."

"I won't let anyone see me." She took a deep breath. "Can we...? Will you...? I don't want anyone to know."

"Staying pure for whomever *el Patrón* chooses." Saying the words did something to me. Even the thought of another man touching her caused my blood to heat.

"I don't want that." Her smile faded. "I've considered leaving."

I cupped her cheek. "You're safe as long as you're in college."

Camila shrugged. "Catalina was, but I don't know about me. Mama said she's doing her best." She tilted her face to my touch. "You know how much a woman's opinion is regarded in securing the cartel."

My forehead furrowed. "You said you haven't been promised."

"I don't know. I wouldn't know until the deal was done." She inhaled, stepped away from my touch, and stood tall. "I've saved some money. Being out in the

74

world on my own is a terrifying thought, but so is being forced to marry a stranger."

Pressing my fist to my chest, I swore my oath. "Camila, you have my word—my promise—what happened tonight stays between us."

Camila nodded. "I promise too." Her smile returned. "I don't want my father to kill you."

"That would really fuck up the alliance." I shrugged. "Of course, if Dario knew what I did, he might give your father permission."

Her lips curled. "What we did, Dante. To avoid your bloodshed, we won't tell anyone."

Our fingers found one another's as if they needed to feel the other. I lifted her hand to my lips. "Thank you for choosing me. You should go back upstairs."

"Okay."

"There's a camera in the elevator."

Camila stiffened. "Shit."

"I figured you didn't know."

"I didn't," she said, fidgeting toward the doors.

Reaching out, I rubbed her slender shoulder. "I'll try to get to the security footage tonight and erase your coming and going."

"What if Dario already saw it?"

"He wouldn't. It would be Giovanni, and if he did, I'll swear him to secrecy." I reached into my pocket. "You need to return the card before Contessa realizes it's gone." My pocket was empty. "Shit."

Camila's grin grew wider as she pulled the card from her pocket. "For a dangerous Mafia guy, you're pretty easy to pickpocket."

Damn—I was impressed.

I shook my head. "You little thief."

"Better than being called a little girl."

"How did you learn to do that?"

"You had me distracted," she said. "I almost forgot to take it back."

"Yeah, you had me distracted, too."

"My brother showed me how when I was about fifteen. My parents used to keep the liquor cabinet locked, but our housekeeper, Lola, always had a key with her. One day, I caught Em with a bottle from the cabinet. He convinced me not to turn him in. In exchange, he'd teach me how to get the key and how to put it back."

"Did Lola ever figure it out?"

Camila shook her head. "We were good. I don't like liquor, but I've found that sometimes, it's helpful to be able to take something without anyone knowing."

I thought of a question. "Is Catalina a pickpocket too?"

"No, she doesn't know. Catalina was always the perfect daughter—you know, the one who agreed to marry because she'd been told to? She might not have turned us in to our parents, but we never let her know."

"To keep this secret" —I motioned between us— "when we see each other..."

Camila nodded. "I know. We can't acknowledge what happened. I'll keep my memory of tonight to myself. It was my choice, Dante. I have the feeling you'll be a hard act to follow."

I didn't want anyone to even try. The idea made my jaw clench.

Camila flashed the card before the sensor and the elevator doors opened. "Good night."

"Good night."

For a moment, I stood watching the doors close. Once I figured she was up to the penthouse, I went to my tablet and accessed the security footage from the elevator. It only took me a few seconds and the evidence was gone.

Looking down at my shorts, I adjusted my still-erect cock and saw a dark spot of moisture.

Evidence of her essence and sweet cinnamon scent remained.

CHAPTER
EIGHT

Camila
Nearly five months later

Mama and I were back in San Diego. Our trip to Kansas City lasted a little less than two weeks. Thankfully, after the first week, our imprisonment by Dario's decree was lifted. That didn't mean that we women were free to go wherever and whenever we chose. It meant that as long as Miguel or one of Dario's men were with us, we could leave the confines of the apartment. Even a luxurious home can second as a gilded cage.

Back at home, Papá and Em increased our security while we were gone. Doors and windows were monitored with alarms, and outside there were motion detectors, cameras, basically anything that money could buy.

Recently, I'd started my second year of college at

SDSU. With Miguel ever present, I wasn't having the same college experience as other women my age. Truthfully, when I looked at the guys in my classes, I saw boys. Growing up around the soldiers and guards of the cartel had shaped my view of what a man should be. There wasn't anything wrong with a studious man who preferred sports to violence. For most women, they were probably a better choice.

My mind told me that men not armed to the teeth were also kinder, yet my experience told me another thing. I knew what my father, uncles, brother, and cousin did, and still, I knew they loved me. Papá wasn't above corporal punishment. That never nullified his love for his children.

When it came down to it, a young twenty-something lanky guy who played tennis and video games didn't garner my interest. After Dante's kiss, I couldn't imagine any of their lips on mine or tongues in my mouth.

It was totally inappropriate the number of times I'd relived that kiss, the sensation of his strong and powerful hands holding me against him, and the hardness of his erection against my core. The force of his lips taking what I offered still sent my blood ablaze.

Just as it had happened that night, the memories caused my panties to dampen. No matter how much I tried and even with a vibrator, I hadn't been able to recreate the orgasm he brought on. And try, I have.

Despite my college experience being different than the average twenty-year-old student, it didn't take away from the fact I was now a sophomore in college. I wasn't completely alone. My cousin Sofia and her friend Liliana, both now living with Aunt Marie and Uncle Nicolas, were also students at SDSU. Sofia almost had the credits to be a sophomore, while Liliana was only beginning her courses.

Catalina and Mireya paved the way as some of the first females in the Roríguez cartel to attend college. Thanks to them, Sofia, Liliana, and I were able to pursue our interests. While it may not seem like a big deal, for us it was. I'd just finished my CAD class, computer-aided design. Normally, my mind would be filled with thoughts and designs. However, today was different.

As I climbed the staircase with my backpack in tow, I tried to subdue my smile. On our way home, Miguel informed me that Papá wanted to see me in his office to discuss something important. Unlike when my sister was similarly summoned, I knew what Papá wanted to discuss. I needed to pretend ignorance. From what I learned, what he's about to tell me was almost announced a few weeks ago, when Aléjandro and Mia had a housewarming party. However, as the gathering was also a celebration of our new niece, Ariadna Gia and we received the announcement that Mia was expecting, Dante shared with me in secret whispers that our news was sidelined—temporarily.

A wave of warmth flowed through me as I thought back to a night over a month ago.

The cartel women were gathered at Aunt Maria's home. There was something big happening within the Roríguez cartel. Aléjandro and el Patrón *wanted the women together and guarded. While being imprisoned under the guise of protection irritated me, I had no choice. Mama and Aunt*

Maria were back in Kansas City to meet my new niece, Ariadna Gia. My cousin Mireya welcomed not only me, but also Liliana and Sofia from Northern California and the newest member of the Roríguez cartel women, Mia Roríguez.

When Mireya and I greeted Mia, the last person I expected to see was Dante. Whatever was happening obviously included the famiglia. My heart beat erratically when his dark eyes met mine. I recalled our agreement to act as if nothing had happened, yet my body had a mind of its own.

There was no comparison between Dante Luciano and the guys in my classes. Wearing a custom suit and a formidable expression, Dante was Mafia danger personified. His razor-sharp jaw, protruding brow, and firm lips made my core twist. His suit accentuated the hard muscles I'd felt months ago, the ones that pushed against my softness. I stared at his impeccably combed hair, remembering what it was like to run my fingers through his locks.

While he didn't say a word, I was barely standing, my breath taken away.

At one point in the evening, while the other ladies were out back on Mireya's patio chatting, I made my way inside the house.

I slipped silently through the hallways toward Uncle Nicolas's office, hoping to catch a glimpse of Dante Luciano. As I turned a corner, I ran face-first into a solid wall of muscle. Dante's hand covered my lips before I could vocally release my surprise. With a twist, he turned the two of us until we were hidden in the alcove of a doorway.

My heart slammed against my breastbone at the sensation of his strong hands on me, holding me in place. My *panties dampened as the leather and spice scent of his cologne brought back a flood of memories. Without thinking, I pressed up on my tiptoes, eager to repeat the kiss we'd shared in Kansas City.*

Dante stiffened as his deep voice sent a chill reverberating through me. "I'm standing in the home of one of el Patrón's *top lieutenants. You will get me killed."*

"I promise, getting you killed isn't my goal."

Dante looked from side to side, and opened the closed door, taking us both into a dark room. It was Uncle Nicolas's empty den. I knew he was at Jano's house with the others; still, the lack of light was unnerving. Dante's warm hand cupped my cheek. "I wanted to talk to you."

My vision adjusted, bringing Dante's handsome silhouette into view. "You did?"

"Camila, I know I'm too old for you."

"You're not," I protested. "Dario and Cat..."

"My sister wasn't happy when she learned she was to marry Aléjandro. She's called out Dario on the misogynistic way marriages are arranged."

"Why are you telling me that?"

"Because Dario mentioned that your name has come up regarding marriage."

Tears came to my eyes. "I haven't been told anything."

"Nothing is set..." In the darkness, the air shifted as Dante lowered himself before me, holding both of my hands in his. Before I could question it, his baritone tenor filled my ears. "You don't know me, Camila. This isn't fair to you, but after what happened...being your first kiss...I want to ask you to marry me."

"Ask me?" My mind couldn't compute. This wasn't the

way things were done in the cartel and especially not with the Mafia.

"If you say yes, I promise I'll move heaven and earth to receive your father's approval."

"My father isn't the only one who will need to approve."

"You're right." He brought my hands to his firm lips and kissed my knuckles. "The only approval I care about is yours. Camila, will you marry me, not for the alliance but because you want to?"

This had to be a dream.

My knees gave way as I too fell to the soft rug. Freeing my hands, I brought them both to his cheeks, his whiskers abrading my palms and sending a twisting sensation to my core. "You're asking me? You want to marry me?"

He lowered his forehead to mine. "Since that night in my apartment, I can't get you out of my head. You're beautiful and smart. You have the courage to go after what you want. You have a fire like your sister that burns twice as bright. I'm not a good person. I won't lie to you. I don't deserve you, but fuck yes, I want you."

"I want you too."

He covered my hands with his. "I want to kiss you, but I don't want anyone to know that you've been kissed."

Gently, I leaned forward until our lips touched.

It wasn't even close to the kiss back in his apartment. But he was right. My lips were swollen and tender after that kiss. I had all night to let them get back to normal. Soon, I'd need to go back with the other women, and I couldn't do that with freshly kissed lips.

Despite the lack of pressure, a moan escaped my lips as

Dante kissed me back. The butterflies returned, fluttering in my stomach and tightening my core.

"I'll speak to Dario first. He's all about the alliance. Hopefully, el Patrón *and your father agree.*"

"I'll act surprised."

Taking a deep breath and nodding at my father's guard Sergio, I knocked on the large double doors to Papá's home office. His deep voice bid me entrance. When I opened the door, I was surprised to see Mama standing near Papá's chair, her expression solemn. "Is everything all right?"

"*Sí,*" Papá said, motioning to the chair opposite his desk. "*Sentarse.*"

Following my father's command, I took the chair, sitting on the edge and settling my backpack on the floor to my side. His gaze swept over my ripped jeans and tank top. I hadn't had a chance to change since my afternoon classes.

"Camila, you're aware of what has happened within the cartel?"

I nodded.

Everyone knew that Uncle Gerardo had betrayed *el Patrón*. It caused a big shake-up. And while Uncle Gerardo wasn't my favorite person, I wasn't happy to learn of his demise. From what Em has said, the change caused a void in Northern California where he had been in charge. *El Patrón's* son Rei was filling in for now.

Papá cleared his throat. "Catalina was able to finish her schooling before she was betrothed." He reached for Mama's hand. "That had been our plan for you too."

Mama looked as if she were about to cry.

"It will be all right, Mama," I consoled.

Her green eyes glistened. "We have insisted that you are able to continue school."

My cheeks twitched with the urge to grin. I'd finish school in Kansas City, with Dante, Catalina, and Ariadna Gia. "You want me to marry?" I did my best to sound surprised.

Papá stood, keeping his broad shoulders back. "With what has happened, it's best to show that those in charge are stable. A married man is respected even by those older. You see, *el Patrón* has decided that Reinaldo will remain in charge of Northern California."

"Rei?" I gripped the arms of the chair as the floor fell out from below me. "Why are we talking about Rei?"

"He and Jano carry a heavy burden," Papá explained, "especially after Gerardo."

This conversation wasn't making sense. My shock wasn't a performance. This wasn't how it was supposed to happen.

"What does Rei have to do with me marrying? What about the alliance with the famiglia?" I asked.

"The alliance is still strong. Currently, *el Patrón* believes we need to show the strength within the Roríguez cartel."

"Oh, Camila," Mama said, coming around the desk to me. "Were you afraid that you'd have to marry into the famiglia?" She crouched down before me and reached for my trembling hand. "No, darling. We said one daughter to them is enough. Jorge has chosen you for Rei. You see, Rei has Gerardo's mansion. It's an honor to be selected to be his wife."

Rei Roríguez's wife.

No.

It took all my control not to scream.

I pulled my hand free. "I don't want a mansion. I don't want to marry Rei."

"It is your duty," Papá said sternly. "Especially after what Gerardo did, we need to unite the Ruizes with the Roríguezes. There was a time *el Patrón* discussed a marriage between Aléjandro and Catalina."

The idea made my stomach roil.

Papá continued, "Another marriage between the cartel and famiglia right now wouldn't be wise. It's a tense situation among some of the soldiers, especially those in the North. They need to see that we're strong on our own, too."

Mama lowered her forehead to my knee. "Camila, you can do this." She looked up through her long lashes. "Rei, he's a good boy."

"He's not a boy. He's a man." I wanted to say that I didn't know him, but I did. During the months he and Jano lived in our pool house, I got to know him. "Mama, I don't hate Rei, but I don't love him. I don't want to marry him."

She stood. "We know this is sudden."

"Does Rei know about this?" My volume rose. "Does he even want this?"

"Of course," Papá reassured. "To wed the drug lord's son is an honor. And you are a respectable woman from our strong family."

"When?"

"The date isn't set," Mama said. "At the end of this semester. Christmas time."

I shook my head. "This isn't happening. I should have some say."

Mama tilted her head.

"I have to transfer my classes." My mind swirled with the logistics of a move I didn't want to make as I babbled about unimportant details.

"*Sí*, it will be worked out," Papá said, retaking his seat behind the desk.

I squared my shoulders. "What if I'm in love with someone else?"

Papá's dark stare zeroed in on me as Mama gasped and stood. Her voice was strong. "You will learn to love Rei."

Tears stung the back of my eyes as I stood. "I don't want this to happen."

"Ca-mi-la," Mama elongated my name.

"My decision is made," Papá said as my phone rang from my backpack. "Who is it?"

I reached down, fumbling for my phone. "Have I lost all my freedoms?"

Papá's gaze hardened. "Who is on the phone? You said you're in love. Is it a boy from the university?"

I read the screen. "It's Catalina." I turned the screen toward him. "Does she know? May I talk to her, or do I need Rei's permission?"

Papá huffed. "Talk to your sister. She will help you."

My sister.

Could Catalina help me?

CHAPTER
NINE

Camila

With my pulse racing, I ignored the weary stares of my parents, hit the green icon, and lifted my backpack from the floor. In the few minutes since I'd lain it down, the bag had tripled in weight. Maybe it was the heaviness of my future that I was feeling. "Cat, *espere por favor*," I said, keeping my eyes downcast and making my way out of Papá's office.

Rushing past Sergio, I sprinted toward my bedroom. The home where I'd lived all my life was but a blur. Once inside my bedroom, I slammed the door and turned the lock. I wasn't under the misconception that a simple knob lock would keep my father or his guards out of my room if they wanted in. I just hoped the lock would be respected.

"Cat" —emotions bubbled in my voice— "do you know?"

"Are you alone?"

I froze and my chest seized at the sound of the baritone tenor, the one I immediately recognized. As I tried to form words, the dam broke on my emotions, tears spilling from my eyes and my voice cracking as I uttered his name. "Dante?"

"I wanted to talk to you before you were given the news."

My temples throbbed from the concoction of emotions. "Papá just told me. I don't want to marry Rei. I want..."

"The next word better be *me*. You want me."

I nodded despite the fact he couldn't see me. "It is you, Dante. I want you."

"Tell me that's your honest reply, and I'll move heaven and earth to make you mine."

Closing my eyes to the familiarity of my pink-painted walls as well as the pictures and posters I loved, more tears cascaded down my cheeks. "I never thought I wanted to marry, not until you."

"This isn't over, Camila. Not by a long shot."

My hands trembled as I held tight to the phone, sat on the end of my bed, and lay back, staring up at the slowly whirling ceiling fan. "Papá said it was set" —I didn't want to say it aloud— "with Rei."

"Fuck, I wish I was with you in California. This is a mistake. I had both Jorge's and Dario's approval."

"You did?" I sat up. "What happened? How did this go so wrong?"

"I don't know. I agreed to all the stipulations."

"Stipulations?"

"Mostly that you could continue working on your degree. I don't want to stop your dream."

"Right now," I said, "it feels like my dream has been ripped away."

"Will you trust me?"

"I want to."

"I'll make this right."

"What can I do? I told my parents I'm" —did I want to admit this?— "I'm in love with someone else. Not Rei. They didn't care."

Before Dante could respond, an explosion of voices erupted at his end of the call. Holding my breath, I waited.

"Dante?"

"Camila, it's me."

The sound of my sister's voice caused a smile to come to my lips. "Cat. Can you help us?"

"I don't know. I didn't know. Why didn't you tell me?"

Why didn't I tell her?

I didn't tell her or anyone because Dante was my impossible dream. A man so incredibly handsome, simply looking his direction caused my core to twist and my panties to dampen. A man with the edge of danger who was also kind and funny. When he looked at me, I felt like I was all he could see, his whole world, despite the Mafia's demands on his time.

Even my thoughts were insufficient to describe the way he made me feel. From the first time I saw him, the night before Cat and Dario's wedding, I was enamored. After my first visit to Kansas City, I was awestruck. However, it was after our first kiss, after I shamelessly rubbed against his body made of hard muscles that I knew my heart had made its choice.

"Camila?"

I concentrated on the noise behind my sister. "Are Dario and Dante arguing?"

The noise disappeared. "They're discussing."

"Me. They're discussing me."

Cat's voice came through without the background noise as if she'd moved away from the men or they'd moved away from her. "Dario told me that Dante requested you. I was afraid you didn't know about it."

"That's what Mama said. She was afraid to let another daughter go to the famiglia. Cat, I love Dante. I think I do. I want to marry him, not Rei."

"Rei is closer to your age."

The lunch I'd eaten long ago churned in my stomach. "You're encouraging me to consider Rei?"

"It's nothing you can consider. Papá went to Jorge when he heard about Dante's proposal. *El Patrón* agreed to change his mind. He recognizes that the cartel needs to focus on its inner strength. After what Gerardo did, your marriage to Rei will reaffirm the Ruiz commitment to the cartel. You'll help Papá's and Uncle Nicolas's standing."

"Their loyalty should speak for itself. I don't want to be a bargaining chip, something to cement their loyalty."

"Camila, Rei is nice. Aléjandro has shown a different

side of himself to Mia. I believe if he can be a good husband, Rei can too."

"I told you."

"You didn't," she protested. "If you had, I could have helped. Mama thought she was doing what was best for you."

I shook my head. "No, the day of your engagement party. Remember?"

"You didn't even know Dante then."

Swallowing, I took a deep breath. "I told you that I didn't want to marry because Papá or *el Patrón* said I should. I wanted to marry for love."

Catalina exhaled. "Love and lust are two different things."

Springing to my feet, I clenched my teeth. "You don't think I know what love is? You think I'm too young."

"Camila..."

"No, Cat. I saw that Dario loved you before you were willing to see it. I might be young, but I know what love is. I know that the stolen moments Dante and I have shared were more than lust."

"What?" her voice was hushed. "What have you two done? Oh Lord. If Papá finds out..."

"We kissed. That's it." Mostly. He also gave me the best orgasm of my life. "I wanted to decide who I would share my first kiss with. I chose Dante and I'm choosing him again." When Cat remained quiet, I added, "The day of your engagement party, you told me that if you and Em had a say in my future, I could...I could marry for love. You're married to the capo dei capi. Help me. Help us."

. . .

DANTE

THE EDGE of Dario's jaw was sharp as the muscles in the side of his face flexed. "You shouldn't be calling her and especially not by using my wife's phone."

"You told me Camila was mine. What the fuck, Dario? You said it was set."

His words came from between clenched teeth as he watched Catalina take her phone and walk toward the library. "Watch your tone. You may be my brother, but I'm your capo."

"Then fix this."

"Tell me why you used Catalina's phone."

"I don't have Camila's number."

Dario ran his hand down his face. "Andrés Ruiz changed his mind after Reinaldo made his intentions known."

"So what? You have more power. You're his son-in-law. You're the capo dei capi."

"Fuck," he roared. "Come with me." He led me toward his office. Once we were inside, he went on. "I know all that. The decision wasn't about you. It's about the Ruizes. After the shit Gerardo pulled, they're nervous that Jorge could change his mind about who he trusts. He trusts his son, both of his sons. By marrying Camila off to Rei, the Ruizes are officially part of the Roríguez family, not just the cartel."

"Nicolas Ruiz has a daughter. What about her?"

"Reinaldo became infatuated with Camila while living at her house."

My blood warmed, and I balled my fingers at my sides. "How infatuated? Did he fucking touch her?"

My brother held up his hand before walking back to his tall leather chair behind his desk. "You know the Ruiz women have the same rules as the women in the famiglia. Reinaldo didn't touch her. If he did, there'd be bigger problems in the cartel."

"I fucking asked her to marry me."

Dario spun toward me, his dark stare scrutinizing me. "You asked her—Camila? You proposed? What the fuck is wrong with you?"

"Nothing is wrong. I want her and respect her ability to make her own choice."

His dark gaze narrowed. "When did you propose?"

"In California, the night the shit went down. Before I asked you to arrange our marriage."

"You talked to her before talking to me?"

I pressed my lips together. "She should be able to make her own decision."

"That's not how the cartel or famiglia works."

Shaking my head, I tried to make sense of this turn of events. "You know, it's your fault."

"How the fuck is it my fault?"

"You brought Camila to me through Catalina. I wasn't looking for a sweet, smart, sexy woman to be part of my life. Hell, I thought I might be the never-marrying type." Letting out a breath, I fell back into one of the chairs opposite Dario's desk. "I noticed Camila the weekend of your wedding. Who wouldn't notice her?" I recalled the way she looked in the bridesmaid dress. "I thought she was too young, too innocent, too..." I stretched out my arm and flexed my fingers. "Not right for a man like me.

"And then I watched you and Catalina. And Camila came here to visit. I had a hard-on during most of those dinners."

"Shit, Dante...don't say that."

"It's the truth. Her vigor. Her excitement about everything. In our dark fucking world, she was a vibrant ray of sunshine. She would have been annoying if she wasn't so sincere. I mean, yes, she's beautiful, but that's only the icing on the damn cake. Despite her age or lack thereof, she knows what she wants, and she goes for it."

"Her schooling?"

"Me."

Dario furrowed his forehead. "You didn't fuck her." His voice rose. "Shit, tell me you didn't touch her."

"We've kissed. A few times. I haven't fucked her although I wanted to."

Dario's nostrils flared as he shook his head. "Here's how it will be, Dante. Choose another bride; you're the underboss of Kansas City. Fuck, you can have any woman in the famiglia or the extended territories. New York has more than a few beautiful women. Italians, women Mom will approve."

"I can honestly say that Mom is not part of this equa-tion. Besides, she didn't fight you with Mia and Aléjan-dro. She doesn't get a vote."

"Fine, there are other women in the Roríguez cartel.

Any woman, I'll make her yours. Any woman except Camila."

"I want Camila." I stood. "I promised her forever. She wants me. Andrés and Valentina thought they were helping her by shutting down my offer and marrying her to Reinaldo. They need to understand that I'm who their daughter wants."

My brother shook his head. "It's out of my hands. If Reinaldo were anyone else's son, but he's not. Fuck, he's Jorge's son."

Standing, I squared my shoulders. "I'm going to San Diego."

"No, you're not. We have shit happening here. I need you here."

"Then bring Camila to me."

Dario exhaled and tipped his chin down. "Twenty-four hours. Make your case to Andrés and Valentina, but don't you dare fuck up this alliance. I have a daughter out there" —he pointed toward the doorway— "who is half-famiglia and half-cartel. You aren't starting a war in my family."

"Twenty-four hours," I agree. "Antonio will watch over Emerald Club. Carmine and Salvatore can handle the streets." Our uncles had reservations about Dario taking charge of the famiglia, but they could see the results. He was leading us. "I'll make a few calls to the capos. Myshkin's people have been quiet of late. Kansas City will stay safe."

My brother stood and walked toward me. His attire showcased his authority, the custom suit as opposed to my dark jeans and black t-shirt. He stood slightly taller than me. "I care about your happiness, Dante." His large hand landed on my shoulder. "You know I do. I don't want a war with Jorge Roríguez. I gave him my word."

I gave Camila my word—my promise.

"Twenty-four hours."

I closed Dario's office door as I stepped toward the foyer. Catalina's voice was coming from the library. After a quick look toward the closed office door, I hurried toward Catalina. She looked up as I entered. Ariadna Gia was in her arms.

"I thought you might still be on the phone."

"Dante," she sighed, looking down at her daughter and back to me. "I'm sorry. I wish I knew how the two of you felt."

"I'm going to have her."

"*El Patrón* has made his decision."

"It's the wrong decision. I'm going to California."

Her green eyes, similar to her sister's, opened wider. "What are you going to do?"

"Keep my promise. I need something from you."

Catalina reached into the pocket of her dress and pulled out a small piece of paper. "Is this what you need?"

I reached for the paper and unfolded it. Camila's phone number was written on it. "Thank you. Does this mean we have your support?"

"It means I want you both to be happy, but the repercussions of this union, of stopping Rei, may be more than our family can withstand."

Closing my fingers around the paper, I leaned down

and brushed Ariadna's soft dark peach-fuzz crown with my lips and smiled at Catalina. "I have to try."

CHAPTER

TEN

Dante

With the time difference between Kansas City and San Diego and a three-hour flight, my plane landed only a little over an hour after I took off. It was just past seven in the evening. The autumn sky was still blue with the beginning crimson hues that came along the horizon with the setting of the sun.

If I was going to succeed in my fight to get Camila, I needed an alliance of my own.

Securing a rental car, I made my way through the increasingly familiar streets to my sister and brother-in-law's house, calling her on the way to be sure she was home. Silas, the head of her security, opened the gate. After I parked, he met me at the door.

"Mr. Luciano."

"Silas, good to see you again. I hope my sister is available."

"*Sí*." He motioned toward the living room. "Come in."

"Dante," Mia exclaimed as she came forward with her arms wide and a stunning smile, an expression unlike she ever displayed during her first marriage. Her light brown hair was pulled back into a low ponytail. Wearing white capris and a bright green top, her hazel stare gleamed with happiness.

I brushed her cheek with a kiss. "How are you feeling?" I looked down toward her midsection, still not showing a baby bump. "And how is my niece or nephew?"

Taking my hand, she led me into the living room to her sofa. The glass doors facing the Pacific Ocean were opened wide and the sound of the surf down below created a soothing rhythm. "I'm tired. Not as tired as I was in the first trimester. And our *bebé* is growing." She narrowed her eyes. "What brings you to San Diego? I didn't know you were coming until you called a few minutes ago."

"It was kind of a last-minute decision." I looked around. "Is Aléjandro here?"

"No. He and Em are off somewhere doing something." She smiled. "He really is more informative than that, but with my pregnancy brain, I'm happy if I can keep my own schedule straight. The school, the one you helped me buy, has seventeen residents. I was there most of the day. We have a full-time tutor."

Mia's joy was contagious.

"That's wonderful. Don't overdo in your condition."

"I'm healthy. I'm excited to make a difference." She sat taller, pulling one leg up to her chest. "We have room for more residents. I think these first ladies are testing the waters for the others." She shook her head. "It's much better living conditions than they've had in the past." She tilted her head. "Enough about me. Why did you say you're here?"

A woman I recalled was named Viviana appeared. "Mr. Luciano, *Señora* Roríguez, may I get you anything? Something to drink?"

We both declined. Once we were again alone, I told Mia what had happened. During her party only a few weeks ago, I was under the impression that everything regarding Camila and me was set.

Her smile faded as Mia laid her hand over mine. "Dante, I'm sorry."

"Don't be fucking sorry." I stood and paced before the open wall as the western sky filled with red, orange, and purple hues. "If Camila didn't know about our marriage, it would be one thing. I'd still want her. But she knows, Mia. I told you that night that I'd asked her. I made her a promise of forever, and now, without my knowledge, it was taken away."

"It isn't like Jorge to change his mind."

"I'm under the impression that it was Andrés who instigated the change."

Pressing her lips together, my sister nodded.

"What do you know?"

Exhaling, she lowered her chin to her chest and looked up at me through her lashes. "Don't do that to me, Dante. I'm not a famiglia spy. I can't relay what I know in confidence from the cartel."

"You know something."

Mia raised her chin. "I've heard talk. Aléjandro was informed."

"Fuck. When?" I sat back on the sofa at her side. "Listen, I'm not asking you for information on products or weapons. I want to know why Andrés Ruiz pulled the rug out from under me with Camila. You know damn well they wouldn't have done this to Dario."

Mia nibbled her lower lip. "In a way they did. How is he taking it?"

"Are you kidding? With Ariadna Gia he doesn't want any waves with the cartel."

She laid her hand over her midsection. "I understand that."

"Camila and I would be another brick in the alliance."

"Not if Andrés has nixed it."

"Nixed it for his own fucking good. He's using his daughter to cement his future with Jorge."

Mia stood. "Yes, like Dario used me and Andrés used Catalina. It fucking sucks, Dante, but that's the world we live in. Dario and Catalina are doing well. So are Aléjandro and I. Camila will adjust. She won't even need to leave the world and culture she knows. Besides, Rei's a good man."

Inhaling, my chest felt tight. "Fuck that. I'm sick of

people singing his praises." My voice rose. "You of all people. I thought you'd see my side in this—Camila's side."

"Me, who has been married off twice in her life?"

"You, who has been preaching against the misogynistic ways men use women. I didn't set out to fall for Camila. I know she's too young for me. I know the shit I've done and will do in the future. I don't deserve her, but that doesn't fucking matter because when I chose her, she chose me too."

My sister's smile returned. "That's right. You're a rebel."

Standing, I clenched my fists at my side. "A lot of fucking good it did me." I spun toward Mia. "I'm going to go talk to Andrés, in person. Man to man."

"*Hombre a hombre.*"

We both turned to the sound of Aléjandro's voice.

"*Qué pasa?*" His eyes narrowed and his forehead furrowed. "It's awfully loud in here for a conversation with your sister."

"You're right," I admitted. "Mia, I apologize." My attention went to Aléjandro. "What changed? Why does Reinaldo want Camila?"

"She's a beautiful woman. Rei is closer to her age. *Mí padre* thinks it's a better pairing." He walked to Mia and after kissing her softly, wrapped his arm around her waist. "Mia has opened my eyes to the importance of creating healthy relationships."

"Dante isn't Gerardo," Mia said, looking at her husband. "Not all age gaps are bad."

"*Sí*, I married an older woman."

Pink filled my sister's cheeks.

"Does he love her?" I asked.

Aléjandro shrugged. "He hasn't used that word. I don't know about you and Dario, but Rei and I weren't exactly raised to recognize the intangibles of feelings and love."

"That's not true," Mia interjected. "Your mother raised you—"

"*Sí*, I stand corrected. However, results, money, power, prestige, those were emphasized."

"And who is getting the power and prestige in that pairing—Rei or Camila? No. Andrés."

Aléjandro didn't respond.

I stood taller. "How about your word? Is that important?"

My brother-in-law squared his shoulders, facing me, challenging me. "We Roríguezes keep our word."

Bring it on. I kicked your ass once. I'll do it again.

My fingers itched to pull the blade from my leg holster. Instead, I worked to keep things civil. After all, now Aléjandro was my brother-in-law. Pulling a knife on him in my sister's home wouldn't help Dario's precious alliance or my chances to wed Camila. "Then stand behind that. Jorge approved of Camila's and my wedding. I gave her my word. I intend to keep it."

Aléjandro's stare narrowed. "Andrés wants Camila to marry Rei."

"Is he—Andrés—a liability? Like Gerardo was?"

"I've known Andrés all my life."

"You knew Gerardo."

Aléjandro pressed his lips together. "Your point?"

"Is Andrés's status within the cartel that threatened that he needs to sell his youngest daughter to ensure it?"

"I trust him. But after what happened to Gerardo, I can see why he wants to tighten the connection to *mí padre*."

"I want to talk to him. Come with me." Shit, I didn't know if this was a good idea or not. "Come with me to talk to Andrés and Valentina. They didn't know that Camila and I had—"

"Had what?" Mia asked.

"Spoken...alone. Discussed marriage."

Mia let out a long breath. "Oh, I was afraid..."

"I haven't taken what isn't mine yet." My attention went back to Aléjandro. "Andrés will at least listen to me if you're there. He owes you that respect."

"*Sí.*"

Mia reached for her husband's hand. "*Por favor, ayudarlo. Él nos ayudó.*"

My eyes went back and forth between the two of them. Whatever Mia said had Aléjandro considering my plea.

He looked at his watch. It was after eight at night. Finally, he spoke, "I'll go with you and hear Andrés out."

"Thank you." I grinned. "*Gracias.*"

It wasn't long until we were on our way. Aléjandro drove the two of us in his Porsche.

"Not a lot of room in here," I said as the darkening streets passed by the windows. "No room for guards."

"I don't need guards to visit one of our lieutenants."

"You're sure?"

"Fuck yeah." His grip tightened on the steering wheel. "Are you saying I need one for you...*mi hermano?*"

"You don't need one for me. I was just thinking. If you're so confident in Andrés's loyalty, why does he think he needs to use Camila to keep your and Jorge's confidence?"

"You can ask him."

While I contemplated the discussion I was about to have with Andrés Ruiz, I couldn't help but think about the reason for the talk. Camila.

Would I even be allowed to see her?

Aléjandro pulled his car up to the gate. I recognized the Ruiz home from the times I'd been there. However, it had changed since the wedding. Now there was a man in a guard shack. After the attack, the Ruizes weren't solely relying on technology.

"*Señor* Roríguez," the guard greeted before he asked a question. While I couldn't understand what he said, by the inflection in his voice, I knew it was a question. By Aléjandro's response, I believe he answered in the negative.

I needed to brush up on my Spanish.

The gate opened and Aléjandro drove us through.

"What did you say to him?" I asked.

"I told him that a lovesick fool wanted to speak to Andrés."

"The fuck?"

Aléjandro laughed. "I said Andrés wasn't expecting us, but he wouldn't deny our visit."

Wouldn't deny us because of Aléjandro. I wasn't

under the misconception that I would be welcomed with open arms.

Beyond the gate, the brick-covered driveway led to the front of the house. Unlike the time I left here with Camila and Valentina, there weren't numerous guards patrolling. Apparently, once one made it past the man at the gate, the house was welcoming. I peered up, noticing the not-so-subtle cameras following Aléjandro's car.

He parked on the circular drive and opened his door without saying a word. I caught up to him by the time we reached the steps, and the front door opened.

"Valentina," Aléjandro said with a slight bow.

"*Señora* Ruiz," I greeted.

"Jano *y* Mr. Luciano." She took a step back. "*Por favor entra.*"

The two of them had a quick conversation of which I only caught my name before *Señora* Ruiz apologized to me for not speaking English and led us up the stairs toward Andrés's office.

"*Visitantes*. Andrés, you have visitors," she announced as she opened his office door.

Andrés Ruiz stood. By his expression, I can only imagine he saw us on surveillance. He didn't seem surprised. "To what do we owe this visit?"

I stepped forward and offered him my hand.

After we shook, Andrés motioned toward the chairs opposite his desk. "Please, sit. What do you want to discuss?"

There was no reason to beat around the bush. "Your daughter Camila."

Señora Ruiz halted her retreat, her gaze going between me and her husband.

Señor Ruiz stalled his movements and turned, his fists on the top of his desk. "What about my daughter?"

I remained standing. "She was promised to me. Our union was approved by my capo and Jorge Roríguez. I've come to make that union official."

"Mr. Luciano, I believe you're mistaken."

CHAPTER

ELEVEN

Camila

" Lo lamento, la señorita. Tu padre is in a meeting and requested that you remain in your room."

Standing in my doorframe, I stared at Miguel, my arms crossed over my chest. My wet long hair lay in a braid over my shoulder. After my discussion with Dante and Catalina, I made the mature decision to sulk in my room. That moping lasted beyond dinner.

While I wanted to cry, I was mostly angry.

This situation was exactly where I never wanted to be. Watching women marry men they barely knew was something I swore I would never do. Over the hours as I stared up at my ceiling watching the fan swirl, I realized Mama and Papá thought with Rei they were saving me from that fate. I knew him. On top of that, we were close in age. I think he's only a year older than I.

Instead of sulking, I needed to tell them who I was in love with. A part of me hoped I could change their minds. When I looked at Rei or thought about him, my body didn't react. There wasn't a slow burning deep within me. My lower stomach didn't twist, and my panties didn't dampen. That didn't mean he wasn't a handsome man. It meant I wasn't attracted to him.

Miguel lifted his brows, waiting for my response. Despite the fact I was showered and dressed in a camisole and pajama shorts, Miguel wasn't affected by my lack of clothes. He had been my bodyguard my entire life.

"I need to speak to Mama and get something to eat."

"*Señora* Ruiz is also with your *padre*."

Mama was in the meeting? Who was it with?

Miguel went on, "Food is good. Lola saved you a plate when you didn't go down for dinner. I'll bring it to you."

"What I have to say to my parents is important."

He nodded.

I scrunched my nose. "You know about the wedding plans, don't you?"

"*Sí.*"

"How long have you known?"

"Not long. I was under the impression that other arrangements had taken place. Reinaldo works hard. He will follow closely behind Jano. You could do worse."

I huffed. "Rei isn't a bad person, but I'm in love with someone else. That isn't fair to Rei. Papá may give him my body, but he'll never have my heart." As the words came forth, I thought about Rei. I needed to tell him what I just said to Miguel.

"You say you're in love. Your mother questioned me. I know nothing about a relationship, and I'm with you all the time. I checked your phone. Who is this mysterious love in your life?"

Of course he checked my phone. Nothing was private.

The sting was back to behind my eyes. "You've done your job well, Miguel. My parents can't blame you. Fate put us together on different occasions."

He lifted his brow. "Such as Catalina's wedding?"

The tips of my lips curled. "That was the first time." My pulse sped up as I thought about Dante. "The arrangements you heard about, were they with Dante Luciano?"

"Is he who you think you love?"

I *think*.

I clenched my teeth together. "I know everyone believes I'm too young to know love, but I'm not. Mama married Papá when she was only seventeen years old. I'm twenty."

"And *Señor* Luciano is thirteen years your senior."

"*El Patrón* married Liliana off to Uncle Gerardo, and he could have been her father."

"That marriage worked well," he replied sarcastically.

I pressed my lips together. "Cat. She's eleven years younger than Dario."

"Sometimes we must trust others, must trust that your parents have your best interests at heart. Perhaps they know something about the younger Luciano that you don't know."

"That he's a murderer, a thief, a criminal? Couldn't the same be said about Rei?"

Miguel shook his head. "I'll bring you a plate from dinner. Promise me that you'll stay in your room until *su padre's* guests leave."

I strained to hear voices, but Papá's office was too far away. The doors were probably closed.

"I can slip down the back stairs and avoid Papá's office."

Miguel's nostrils flared. "Stay, Camila. Your father's orders." With that, he turned on his heel, heading toward the back staircase.

Stay.

Sit.

Marry.

I wasn't the daughter of a top lieutenant in the Roríguez cartel; I was a dog, someone who was expected to obey each command. It may be expected, but I hadn't promised. I'd stayed silent.

My grip on the doorframe tightened as my curiosity grew about Papá's meeting. He had meetings all the time. To stay in my room was an unusual request.

It bid the question, why?

Taking one last look down the back hallway to confirm Miguel's descent to the lower level, I stepped from my room, my bare feet padding silently on the decorative runners. My entire life had been spent in this house, so I deftly avoided the boards in the hardwood floor that would make a sound. By the time I reached the landing, my heart was thumping in my ears.

Staying hidden behind the corner where the hallway and loft intersected, I crouched down, watching the area before Papá's office. The doors were closed. If Sergio wasn't standing guard, literally standing, I wouldn't know that Papá had visitors—visitors that also included Mama. Sergio stood when guests were inside. Besides, I had no reason to doubt Miguel.

Sergio turned toward the doors, reaching for a door-knob and pushing it inward. I held my breath as Mama exited, casually looking over her shoulder. I heard a deep voice with a heavier Latino accent than my father's. For a moment, I thought it could have been Jorge.

Aléjandro Roríguez, Jorge's oldest son, stepped from the office, followed closely behind by another man. I saw his boot and jean-clad leg. I anticipated Rei. It would make sense that Papá didn't want me to come out dressed as I am with my future husband here. I sucked in a breath and covered my lips with my fingers to stop myself from making a sound.

The man behind Jano wasn't Rei; it was Dante.

My nipples beaded beneath the silk of my camisole as goose bumps scattered over my arms and legs. I couldn't believe that he was here in my house. Without pause, I scanned from his dark boots up his long denim-covered legs. He wasn't wearing a suit as his brother would. No, Dante was wearing a navy t-shirt over the washboard abs I'd felt the night in his apartment, his muscle-bound arms exposed. His deep tone reverberated through me, sending tingles through my circulation.

Papá was the last to exit as he offered his hand to Jano and then to Dante.

Dante hesitated. "We had an agreement."

"Your agreement was with Jorge, not with me."

"My capo negotiated the arrangement the same as the one with Catalina." Dante squared his shoulders. "I won't stop until I speak with Jorge himself."

"Mr. Luciano," Papá said loudly, "I am Camila's father." His dark eyes flashed toward Jano. "While I respect Jorge, Camila's future is my decision."

"Perhaps my uncles were right to warn us about trusting the cartel. Will this misunderstanding have a ripple effect? Will shipments of product you've promised be rerouted at the last minute?"

"My daughter isn't a product to be sold."

"Then don't sell her for your own gain. Give her to me to be treasured."

Treasured.

My core clenched.

"My decision is final."

"I will alert my capo."

"My daughter's husband," Papá replied. "I'll call him myself."

"We aren't done," Dante said. "I won't be so easily led away. Camila was promised to me."

Papá bowed his head and looked up. "Camila's engagement party is tomorrow. My decision is final."

Tomorrow.

I hadn't been told.

New tears prickled the back of my eyes at the realization Dante flew all the way to California for me. I do know love when I feel it. He loves me too or he wouldn't be fighting for me.

As a large hand squeezed my shoulder, I jumped, bringing my hand to my chest to try to contain my rapid heartbeat.

"Your room," Miguel menacingly whispered near my ear.

I spun around, standing as I turned with my cheeks rising. "He loves me," I whispered. "He's here fighting for me."

Miguel closed his eyes and exhaled. "Child, it would be better if you didn't know. You can't change the future." He tugged my hand. "To your room before you're seen."

Walking down the hallway, I pulled on my upper lip with my teeth.

Miguel was wrong.

The future was the one thing I could change.

Now, how could I contact Dante before he went back to Kansas City.

I had an idea.

Alone in my bedroom with the tray of food from dinner, I found my appetite had disappeared, replaced by a sense of urgency. In my list of contacts on my phone, I searched for Mia's number. I didn't have it. I did have Jano's. Fresh goose bumps covered my skin. I was supposed to marry Jano's brother. Surely, he wouldn't help me pursue Dante. I also had Rei's.

That meant he had mine.

He could have called me about this marriage.

He hadn't.

Dante had flown across the country.

Fourteen steps one direction, sixteen the other. My bare feet padded over my plush carpeting as I paced the confines of my bedroom. Another possibility occurred to me. Quickly, I hit the icon next to Catalina's name in my recent call list.

"Camila."

The deep tone alerted me that Cat hadn't been the one to answer the call. I hadn't considered the time difference until I heard his voice.

"Um, Dario, I'm sorry to call so late."

He exhaled. "Yes, Catalina is with Ariadna right now, trying to get her back down. She can call you in the morning."

Standing tall, I willed myself to be strong. "I called for Mia's number. Could you give it to me?"

"Mia? Is everything all right?"

No.

"I thought I had her number..." I rambled on for a few sentences, not completely certain of what I said when Dario finally gave in, probably to get me off the phone.

I wrote the number on a notepad on my desk.

"Thank you, Dario."

"Camila" —his tone was softer— "sometimes things don't seem like they work out, but in the long run, it's for the best."

"I believe things can work out. Good night." I disconnected the call and dialed the number I'd just written down.

Mia answered on the second ring. I spoke low and fast, unsure if she was on my side or not. Truthfully, when all was said and done, we would be sisters-in-law. Whether I married Rei or Dante, our fate was sealed. The only way out of that was me running away.

If I truly hated or even didn't know either possible husband, that might be an option. I knew them both and knew which one I wanted.

With my hopes high, I thanked Mia and disconnected the call.

Now, to check to see if I was behind a closed door or if I had a guard on the other side.

Slowly, I opened the bedroom door.

Miguel's chair was empty.

That didn't give me much time.

CHAPTER
TWELVE

Dante

The drive back to Aléjandro's home was quieter than our ride to the Ruiz home. There were the few minutes when Aléjandro called his father. My observation was that Jorge Roríguez was a man of few words. When Aléjandro questioned the reasoning behind the change from me to Rei, Jorge simply said it was his decision and he stood by it. My brother-in-law may feel sorry for me, but I wouldn't doubt that his loyalties lay with his brother.

He pulled the Porsche into the garage. The slamming of doors echoed throughout the garage, around a large SUV, a black Mercedes, and a sharp Ducati motorcycle.

Mia met us in the kitchen. "It didn't go well." Her voice lacked emotion, as if she could read the anguish on my face.

Instead of answering, I sat in one of the tall chairs at their kitchen island, contemplating my next move. I pulled my knife from its sheath and laid it on the counter before me. Kidnapping was an option, but one that would definitely fuck with the alliance.

I concentrated on the intricacies of the mother-of-pearl and silver handle. This knife originally belonged to *mio nonno* Alessio. He was our mother's father.

When I was young, *Nonno* took me under his wing. He knew what my future held. He knew I'd always be second in everything. Second born. Second son. The underboss, not the boss. The knowledge that the cartel wouldn't have changed plans like this if I were Dario grated on my nerves.

They wouldn't fuck the capo or future capo. The underboss was inconsequential.

Nonno gave me this knife when I was only eleven. I've treasured it. Cared for it. Cleaned my enemies' blood from it. I'd used it for my first kill. My thoughts circled as Mia and Aléjandro spoke.

"I called *mí padre*," Aléjandro explained to Mia, "from the car. Dante heard the same answer from him as he did from Andrés."

"That means it's settled." Mia's tone was softer as she looked at her husband. "Your thoughts?"

"We're in a fucking tight spot," he replied. "Dante" —he jutted his chin my direction— "is your brother. Rei is mine."

"You and Rei are close. Have you heard him talk about Camila?"

"He's said a few things, mostly about her ass and small tits when she's at the pool."

I flicked my wrist.

Mia screamed.

"The fuck?" Aléjandro roared as he followed my knife, pulling it from their kitchen wall.

"Jesus, Dante," my sister scolded.

Aléjandro's dark stare zeroed in on me, silently warning as he handed my knife back butt first.

"Would he fight for her?" I asked, savoring the feel of the cool handle in my palm.

"No one is fighting," Mia said. "I know you don't want to hear it, Dante, but the powers-that-be have spoken."

"You're right. I don't want to hear that."

She turned toward Aléjandro. "Has anyone asked Camila?"

He shrugged.

"I spoke to her."

Mia had my attention. "You spoke to her? Tonight?"

"Yeah, she called me not long ago." Mia turned to her husband. "She likes Rei." She shook her head. "She had no idea there was a wedding planned between the two of them until Andrés told her this afternoon."

"The engagement party is tomorrow," I said through gritted teeth.

"She doesn't want to hurt Rei," Mia went on. "But she's convinced she's in love with" —Mia laid her hand on my shoulder— "this guy."

I turned to Aléjandro. "Do you have some Russian assholes around here? I really need to kill somebody."

Mia laid her hands on her husband's chest, splaying her fingers and looking up at him through her lashes. "Have you ever gone against your father's word?"

He closed his eyes with a mixture of a curse and growl.

She turned to me. "How will Dario take it if you go against his wishes?"

"What do you think? He'll be fucking pissed."

Mia was again talking to Aléjandro. "Healthy relationships involve both parties. Dante and Camila have started that relationship, willingly, consensually. Some arranged marriages work. Hell, Rei and Camila would probably work in the long run, but according to her, there's no fire there. No flames of passion or" —she grinned— "of hatred."

"Yeah, those are fucking hot."

I pointed my knife in their direction. "That's right. I remember. Mia had that contract out on you." My thoughts went to Camila. Fire. There was an inferno the night of her first kiss, her first orgasm in the presence of a man. Damn, the memory caused my balls to draw tight.

Mia spoke. "What's missing in the arrangements the men make is the future bride's input. I got that tonight from Camila."

Aléjandro shook his head. "Andrés said the engagement party is tomorrow, but *mi padre* didn't say anything about it."

"Because," I interjected, "Andrés pulled that out of his ass. I bet if you called Rei, he either just learned about it or hasn't yet been told."

"If you ask me," Mia said, "there's way too much

planning and arranging without involving the parties who are directly affected."

"What are you saying?" I asked. "What is your suggestion?"

She took a deep breath, her gaze going between the two of us. "I'm suggesting that Camila can't be engaged tomorrow if she's married tonight." Mia looked at the clock over the double ovens. "I mean, we need to hurry, but there are still almost two hours left of today."

I jumped from the stool. "Married. I don't have a ring. What about a license?"

"You want to do this?" Aléjandro asked Mia. "You want to piss off *mí padre y tu hermano?*"

"We're encouraging another cartel/Mafia wedding. It's for the alliance." She feigned a smile and laid her hand over her midsection. "And they can't punish me. I'm carrying a *bébe.*"

"I'm not," Aléjandro muttered.

Aléjandro ran his hand over his hair. "I'll call the priest who performed our wedding. Tell him I need a favor."

My blood raced as I listened. Fuck, I thought this was over...and now? My eyes opened wide. "Where is Camila?"

"Oh," Mia said with a giggle. "Yeah, if this is a go, you're supposed to call her with my phone. She should be out of her house. I think she needs a knight on a white horse to go find and save her."

I couldn't contain my smile. "Fuck no. If she's willing to do this, go against everyone, she's fucking saving me.

Give me your phone." I paused, meeting my sister's shining stare. "Why are you doing this?"

Mia let out a breath. "I was a bitch. Well, I wasn't as welcoming to Catalina as I should have been. I realized that when Josefina welcomed me into this family. Camila will be welcomed by the Roríguezes or the Lucianos. She should be where she wants to be."

"Even if it causes a war within the alliance?" I asked.

"A battle, not a war."

Looking down at Mia's phone, I felt the need to talk to Camila. "You said she might be out of her house." My nerves grew taut. "Is she safe?"

"Call her."

As I pushed the icon, Aléjandro made his call to the priest, walking toward his office. Mia hurried down the hallway toward Silas and Viviana's room.

"Dante?" Camila's voice came from the phone, washing through me and taking away the defeat I'd felt not long before.

"I was wondering if you were up for a wedding tonight?"

"Tonight? Mia did it. She got Aléjandro to agree?"

"He's calling the priest right now. Tell me where to find you."

"I'm still in my house."

Good that she's safe.

"Can you get out unnoticed?" I asked. "Fuck, I'll drive up to the gate if I need to."

"I can get out. The new security is..." Her words trailed away. "I can do it."

"Tell me where to meet you."

I quickly typed her instructions into my phone and set my GPS. "I can be there in seventeen minutes." I closed my eyes. "I love you, Camila. We can make this work."

"I love you, too."

As I disconnected the call, I turned, meeting my sister's hazel stare.

"Here," she said, "I have something for you."

Looking down, I watched as her fingers unfurled, revealing a large red ruby on a gold band, with tall prongs.

"No, Mia. That was Nonna Luna's ring, the one that was stolen. You have it back."

She glanced toward the knife still on the counter. "That knife you stabbed my wall with belonged to Nonno Alessio. The knife and ring will be together under one roof as they were when Nonna and Nonno were alive." When I didn't respond, she shoved the ring in my direction. "Take it and go. It's too small for me but should fit Camila. You can take Jano's car."

I slid the ring into my pocket.

Jano's car.

His Porsche.

I'd rather take his Ducati.

"I have my rental car."

Silas and Viviana emerged from their hallway. While Silas was subdued, Viviana was grinning from ear to ear. "We have a wedding tonight. I have some quick baking to do."

Aléjandro came out of his office, shaking his head.

"What?" I asked.

"Father Gallo will be here as soon as he's able. He can perform the ceremony, but he can't make the marriage legal until tomorrow at the courthouse."

Shit.

Fuck.

One step forward and two back.

"It will be blessed," I said, trying to convince myself. "That should appease the famiglia, the *families*." I hoped it would. If the marriage wasn't legal, Andrés could pull some annulment bullshit.

Aléjandro continued, "The priest said there's another option. In California, you can marry online. The two people must physically be present in California and together. He knows of a 24-hour website."

Hope returned.

"We'll do both. Legal through the website and blessed by the priest."

"Go," Mia said. "Go get your bride."

THIRTEEN

Camila

My pajamas were replaced with a pair of shorts, top, and hoodie. If seen by my parents or any of the guards, the change wouldn't incite anyone's curiosity. The long white sundress I have stuffed into my backpack would. It wasn't what I imagined my wedding dress would be, but as my circulation hummed with anticipation, I knew my dress wasn't what I'd remember about this night. It would be the significance of saying 'I do.'

Turning my phone to vibrate, I stuffed it in my back pocket. I zipped my backpack and swung it over my shoulder. Inside my bedroom, I stilled, standing with my hand on the doorknob and looking around.

Seeing the room I'd lived in my entire life, memories stared back at me. Pictures in frames and others pinned to a bulletin board. Hurrying to the bookcase, I grabbed a framed picture of Em, Catalina, and me. It was taken at Catalina's graduation from college. Taken before her life changed forever. The innocence we shared could be seen in our happy and clueless eyes. The time from before tugged at my heart.

I slipped the framed photo into an outer pocket on the backpack.

The rest of the room represented my childhood, the period of time I was walking away from.

I was leaving of my own volition, not acquiescing as Catalina did, a bargaining chip handed over by our father and gifted to the Kansas City Mafia. The fact that I was headed to the same place was insignificant. The truth that I was leaving based on my own desires was what mattered.

Opening my bedroom door, I saw Miguel's empty chair. It was fair to assume he'd gone to his room for the night, assured of my obedience. Soft lights directed at the floorboards on each side illuminated the quiet hallway. Holding my tennis shoes, I walked barefooted, quietly making my way to the back staircase.

The memory of Miguel keeping me safe in this exact spot crushed my chest. He'd be blamed for my absence. My parents would take my disobedience out on him.

"I'm sorry, Miguel," I whispered as I slowly descended the back staircase.

Turning on the midway landing, I stopped walking and listened for noises coming from the kitchen.

Nothing.

My plan was to exit out onto the pool deck, duck

behind the pool house, where the Roríguez men lived for a few months. I knew that hidden along the fence line was a gate leading off the property that allowed the two of them to come and go without dealing with the security.

Slipping through the kitchen, I descended the next set of stairs to the lower level. A quick look at the green light near the glass doors let me know that the sensors were disarmed. Opening the glass door, the sound of the surf from beyond the cliff filled my ears. Darkness encompassed the pool deck and the abyss beyond. Even the stars and moon were obscured in shadows. Only the colorful illumination of the ever-changing hues beneath the pool's crystal-clear water penetrated the darkness.

Keeping myself in the shadows, I slid on my tennis shoes. With one last look at the only home I'd known, I took the path around the pool house. As I reached the tall gate, it opened inward.

My heart forgot to pump as the viscous liquid drained from my face to my feet.

"Where are you going?" my brother asked, eyeing me up and down, his gaze settling on my backpack.

"Em, forget you saw me."

His iron grip came to my wrist as his voice lowered. "Fuck, Camila. You can't fight this. I wish you could. I've done what I could. Cat couldn't fight it. You can't either."

Lifting my chin, I met his gaze. "I'm not fighting. I'm choosing. Please respect that."

His grip loosened. "You're choosing? What the fuck are you choosing, to run away? Don't you think the cartel has the resources to find you? You will be hunted. And what if you're found by the bratva?"

The thought sent a cold shiver over my flesh. I lifted my chin. "I'm not running away. I'm choosing who I'll marry."

Em's dark stare narrowed, drilling into me for an extended moment before he connected the dots. "You're choosing Luciano?"

"I am." I softened my voice. "I love Dante, Em. Please respect that."

"I fought for Rei with Papá." His expression morphed. "You know him. Rei is a good man."

"He is," I agreed. "I'm sorry he got dragged into this. Dante asked me to marry him before talking to Dario and before Dario approached *el Patrón*. I said yes."

Em pressed his lips together. "I'm supposed to be okay with both my sisters leaving our family and moving in with the famiglia?"

"You're supposed to support both your sisters. You supported Cat." I feigned a smile. "I know you gave her lessons to protect herself."

"Should I slide my blade into that backpack?"

"I'd be happy with your blessing."

His nostrils flared. "To marry Luciano?"

"To marry the man I want to marry."

"Do you have any idea how fucking ballistic Papá is going to be when he finds out you're gone?"

I nodded. "That's why you need to say you didn't know anything about it."

"Does Dario know?"

I shook my head.

Em inhaled, his chest pressing against his shirt as he lifted his hand, palm up.

I looked suspiciously at his opened hand. "What are you doing?"

"Who is coming to get you?"

"Please don't fight him, Em."

He repeated his question.

"Dante," I admitted.

"Papá won't be giving you away. Let me take you to him and ensure you're safe until I give you to him."

A lump of emotion formed in my throat as I laid my hand in my brother's.

Em closed his fingers around mine. "I need to tell Luciano that if he hurts you in any way, I don't give a damn about the alliance, I'll fucking hunt him down."

Letting go of Em's hand, I wrapped my arms around his torso. "Thank you."

"Where is he picking you up?"

I told my brother the cross streets.

"Come this way," he said, "I'll help you avoid the cameras."

Under the blanket of darkness, Em led me beyond the gate, around the side of the house, and through the underbrush of our landscaping, skimming neighbors' properties until we came to an opening facing the street, two properties away from ours.

Immediately, the lights flashed from an unfamiliar black sedan. Em reached for his gun as the car slowly rolled toward us. The car stopped, the driver's-side door opened, and two hands came into view.

"Don't shoot."

My heart filled with hope as Dante Luciano stood, his wide shoulders appearing as if they couldn't possibly fit in the small car. His body unfolded. Beneath the shirt I'd seen him wear earlier at my house, I imagined his toned torso. As he stepped around the car, I scanned his long legs. With my knees weak, I dropped my backpack and ran toward him.

When we collided, Dante wrapped his arms around me, and I buried my face in his chest, inhaling his scent of leather and spice. "You came all the way out here to fight for me."

His large palm gently cupped my cheek. "I was willing to do more to fight for you."

Em appeared behind me, my backpack in his hand and his gun no longer in sight.

Dante extended his hand. "Emiliano."

My brother used his dominating tone. "Dante. You realize this is going to cause problems with *el Patrón* and your brother."

Dante nodded. The sharp edge of his chiseled jaw clenched as his Adam's apple bobbed. "We're getting married tonight. Come with us."

Em looked from Dante to me and back. "I don't know what the fucking fallout will be, but I know Camila wants to go with you." He inhaled. "Take care of her, motherfucker. The alliance will survive, but if you hurt her, you won't."

Dante's lips quirked. "Do you give this woman...?"

I took a step away from Dante and turned to my brother.

Em wrapped his arms around me. He then pulled

back and lifted my chin. His next words came in Spanish, keeping them from Dante. "Love you, Camila. Don't shut us out. We're your family."

I replied in the same language. "I love you, too. I won't. I promise."

He continued in Spanish. "Mama will be heartbroken."

That reality tore at my heart. I didn't want to hurt my mother. I hoped that one day she'd understand. "She'll survive."

Em reached for my head, tilting my face down and brushing a kiss to my hair. When I looked up, Em and Dante were in a stare-down. I spoke in English. "Love you, Em. Thank you."

Dante's hand found mine, intertwining our fingers.

I looked up at him. "Let's get married before I'm engaged to someone else."

Dante walked me around the car, opening the passenger door and brushing his lips with mine before I slid into the soft seat. After the door closed, he stopped and spoke to Em. They both nodded before he walked to the driver's door.

As Dante folded himself into the driver's seat, he reached over and took my hand in his. "I can't believe you came up with this plan."

"You came all the way to the West Coast to fight for me."

His nostrils flared. "I failed."

Turning my hand in his until our palms were together, I squeezed his much-larger hand. "You didn't fail, Dante. From now on we're a team. You made the first play. I made the second." Warmth filled my cheeks. "I think that means it's your turn."

He put the car in gear as a sexy smile filled his expression. "I've been thinking about having you alone and to myself since you appeared in my apartment." His dark gaze connected briefly with mine. "I've had plenty of time to imagine all the things I can do to you."

I fidgeted in the seat. "I've been doing the same, but admittedly, my imagination is rather limited in its knowledge."

Dante drove a few blocks before pulling the car over to the side of the road.

"What?" I asked.

Dante leaned toward me. The scent of leather and spice filled my senses as my body warmed. His nose touched mine as his dark stare melted my insides, turning them to a molten lava. Without a word, he unbuckled my seatbelt.

CHAPTER
FOURTEEN

Dante

C amila was so fucking stunning. Within the span of a breath, as I stared into her emerald gaze, prominent memories of our short relationship sped through my thoughts. From seeing her for the first time the night before Dario's wedding and wondering why in the hell he hadn't chosen her, to taking a knee in Nicolas Ruiz's home and asking Camila to marry me. Every stolen moment in between all culminated in having her here now, with me.

As the fast-forward reel spun, a new emotion morphed to life within me. The anger and doubt that had taken residence in my psyche at Andrés's change of plans converted into an overwhelming need to protect the woman in my grasp. Yes, I wanted her naked beneath me, but more importantly, I was keenly aware of the worlds in which we lived. Danger lurked around every corner and in every shadow. Lives were continually lost in cruel and heinous ways.

Those were worlds we couldn't escape. Nevertheless, I could do my best to keep her from the dirty, gritty reality.

Taking Camila away from the cartel wasn't the benevolent move it could appear to be on the surface. No, while I was taking her away from a life drenched in perilous endangerments from threats all around, life in the Kansas City Mafia wasn't exactly safer. If anything, it would be more dangerous. As my wife, Dario's sister-in-law, and a member of the cartel under the Mafia's umbrella, Camila will arrive in Kansas City with a target on her back.

The tenor of my words grated with desire. "Do you know what happened when you chose to get in this car?"

She nodded, causing our noses to brush. "I chose you."

"That means you're mine, Camila."

Camila nodded, this time less confidently. Perhaps the entirety of her decision weighed on her.

Pushing back and inclining my seat, I encouraged her to come closer.

Fucking small car.

Camila obeyed, climbing onto my lap. She peered right and left through the windows. "What if they know I'm gone? What if the guards are coming for me? Shouldn't we leave?"

My hands found their way beneath her hooded sweatshirt to the softness of her skin. I splayed my fingers around her small waist. "You're right." My breathing grew shallow as my circulation rerouted. The zipper of my blue jeans strained with her petite body in my grasp. "I need to kiss you. I need to know you're really here." I moved my palms to her cheeks. "A kiss like I couldn't give you in front of your brother."

Her giggle filled the car. "He was armed."

"So am I."

"Is that what I'm feeling?" She wiggled her sexy ass.

"No," I growled. "Be careful. I could do more than kiss you."

"It is my wedding night."

"Oh fuck," I growled with a grin. "We're breaking enough rules. You'll legally be mine before I take your sweet, tight cunt."

Camila's breathing hitched.

"You do know what will happen after our vows, right?"

She nodded quickly. "With you, Dante. Only with you."

Palming her cheeks, I brought her luscious lips to mine.

Fuck.

My cock hardened from wood to steel as I tasted her sweetness and plunged my tongue into the depths of her warm haven. Her moans and whimpers filled the air as we both sought to get closer. No longer content with holding her face, my hands again wandered...beneath her sweatshirt, beneath the second shirt. Each inch of her flesh was softer than the last.

Pushing the cups of her bra down, I fondled her

breasts, palming each one. The way her back arched and her shriek reverberated in the car was more effective than Viagra as I tweaked each nipple. Camila was all the woman I didn't deserve, and yet, here she was in my grasp.

She didn't back away. No, Camila pressed back, kissing me as if she were kissing to save her life. Her small body wiggled over mine as the scent of cinnamon filled my senses. There was more, the scent of her arousal.

It took all my self-control to keep my touch above her waist. I reminded myself that in the span of a few hours, I'd have access to all of her.

Finally, I pushed her back, only far enough to break our connection. "Fuck, Camila. We need to say our vows. I'm ready to fuck you right here." I ran my thumb over her swollen lips. "You're fucking gorgeous, and I don't deserve you."

Her chin lowered.

"No." I lifted her chin until our gazes met. "You are gorgeous. I've thought so since the first time I saw you." Her long lashes fluttered. "Are you certain of your decision?"

"I am." There was no wavering in her voice.

I pushed the button, raising my seat and helped her climb back to the passenger seat. "Then we have a wedding to attend."

After she fastened her seatbelt, I wiped the condensation from the inside of the windows and peered into the shadows along the street. Camila was right. There could easily be cartel members nearby. I put the car in drive. After adjusting myself, we began the drive to Aléjandro and Mia's home.

A few minutes into the trip, I spoke, "I promise that as mine, you'll be safe and protected." The streets of San Diego passed by the windows. "We're going to have shit to deal with because of our wedding, but I don't want you to worry about it."

She pressed her sexy, swollen lips together. "Tonight is my wedding. I don't want to talk about what will happen later unless it's about what will happen once we're alone." She lowered her chin, and I could only imagine her cheeks filling with a rosy hue. "And maybe we shouldn't talk about that."

Stealing a look in her direction, I grinned. "You don't need to worry about that either."

"I'm not worried. I'm..." She lifted her hands to her face. "After that kiss...I'm curious." She lowered her hands. "I chose you for my first kiss. I'm choosing you for all my firsts."

"I fucking hope you never regret that decision."

"I don't plan on it."

I pulled the rental car up to Aléjandro and Mia's gate and pushed the button. Silas's voice came from the box. "Identify yourself."

"Dante Luciano, Silas."

The gate before us opened.

Camila laid her head against the headrest. "I can't believe we're having a secret wedding at Aléjandro Roríguez's home."

A new thought came to me. "Will you regret not having a big wedding?" I turned to watch her expression.

Camila shook her head. "It's so much. There's too much pressure. I wish my parents were here and supportive, but that was their choice when they wouldn't listen to me." She exhaled. "Honestly, I'm happy to not have all the eyes of the cartel and Mafia on me. Or on our sheets tomorrow morning." She reached over, laying her hand on my arm. "This is better."

I exhaled. "Your parents, Jorge, and Dario...they'll all be upset."

"We're here at Aléjandro's home. He's number two."

"The location implies consent," I said, putting the car in park.

"Does he really support us? If he does, that should help us with *el Patrón*."

"Mia has gotten to Aléjandro. He's supporting us for her."

"I wasn't sure if she'd help me when I called."

I reached for her hand and squeezed. "She's on your side. Having two weddings she didn't want has turned her into an advocate for the woman in these marriages."

"She didn't want to marry Jano? They seemed happy at their housewarming party."

I shook my head. "She didn't want to, but obviously, they worked through it."

Camila looked down. "I suppose things could have worked out with Rei." She looked up, turning to me. "But I don't want him. I want you. I want this."

"Me too."

As we walked toward the house, Camila stopped. "Are my lips...? Will they know we kissed?"

I stared for a moment at her lips, her features. Her

142

lips were pinkened and still swollen. Her vibrant emerald eyes sparkled with anticipation and trust. Camila Ruiz was fragile and breakable. Yet I never wanted her to be broken. My desire was for the whole world to see Camila shine in all her glory. "Let them speculate."

"What if they think we did more?"

"Then I'll kill them."

Her eyes opened wide. "What?"

"No one discusses our sex life or speculates about it. If they do, I'll cut their throats."

"So, no one will look at our sheets tomorrow?"

"No." I meant what I said.

A minute later, we entered Aléjandro's home. Mia was waiting near the entry, smiling at Camila. If she saw anything in Camila's lips, my sister didn't say. Instead, she wrapped my fiancée in a hug. "We're going to be sisters-in-law."

Camila nodded.

Mia went on, "The priest is here, but if you want to go upstairs and get ready, there's time." Mia wrapped her arm around Camila, leading her away. "I've been searching my closet for something that might fit you. I'm obviously bigger than you are..."

Camila smiled over her shoulder as Mia led her up the stairs and their conversation disappeared into the bustle of the first floor.

Silas was out on the pool deck, stringing lights in a make-shift arch.

"Dante," Aléjandro said, placing his hand on my shoulder. "Let me introduce you to Father Gallo."

It felt as though I was in a dream where everything

was in front of me, yet I was watching from far away. I pushed the sensation away and shook Father Gallo's hand. "Thank you for coming so quickly."

The priest went on to explain that the ceremony would cover the religious commitment and then he'd guide us through the online process, making our marriage a legal union.

"Our license will have today's date?" I asked.

"As long as we hurry."

It was already after eleven.

In the kitchen, Viviana was putting the finishing touches on a round cake with white frosting. "How did she make that so fast?" I asked Aléjandro in a whisper.

"She didn't. Silas went out and bought a cake. She's personalizing it."

I met my brother-in-law's gaze. "I'm sure this is difficult for you, the other man being Reinaldo and all."

"Camila wants you."

"And you approve?"

"I approved before Rei was in the picture. I wasn't told about the change of plans until they were set." He hesitated. "There will be unhappy people on both sides. We need to be prepared." He clasped his hand on my shoulder. "Mia and I want you and Camila to spend tonight here." He looked over at a large clock. "It's late and if word gets out, this house is well protected with technology and manpower. If anything happened to Camila, the alliance could end up in a bloodbath."

"You think there could be dissent from members of the cartel?"

Aléjandro nodded. "*Sí*. The alliance is tenuous in the

eyes of some. There was a balance achieved with my marriage. One bride to the famiglia and one to the cartel. Camila was supposed to stay in the cartel. Her marrying you is a blow to that balancing act."

"We have your support?"

Aléjandro inhaled, squaring his shoulders. "*Sí* and my wife's."

I didn't want to risk Camila's safety. "Thank you. We'll stay here." I lowered my voice. "I promised Camila there would be no viewing the sheets in the morning."

My brother-in-law grinned. "Then you're at the right house. That isn't one of your traditions that we uphold."

CHAPTER
FIFTEEN

Camila

S tanding in front of the full-length mirror, I didn't see the same woman who I'd seen hours earlier, back at my house. Gone was the frizzy, braided hair and the bloodshot eyes. The woman in this reflection was radiant, the way I'd always imagined a bride should be.

When we pulled my dress from the backpack, it looked like it had been stowed away in a ball because it had. Mia ironed the long white sundress, erasing the wrinkles and making it crisp. Wearing a pair of Mia's high-heeled shoes, I turned a slow circle, seeing someone new.

The dress was the only item I'd thought to bring. That left me with no makeup or a way to style my hair. Mia offered me the use of her makeup. As I highlighted my eyes, cheekbones, and lips, she curled and styled my hair. She pulled it up on the sides securing it with dainty pearl combs and draping the long dark curls behind my shoulders.

"You're beautiful," she said, standing back and crossing her arms. "Dante is a lucky man."

I met her gaze in the mirror. "Thank you for helping me and making me feel welcome."

Her cheeks rose as she smiled. "I wish I'd done more for Catalina when she and Dario married. I've vowed not to make that mistake again."

I spun toward her. "I know in my heart that I've made the right decision. I hope this doesn't get you and Jano in trouble with *el Patrón*."

"I'll let Aléjandro worry about that." She shrugged. "I'm sure I'll get an earful from my other brother." Her smile returned. "It's a good thing I'm no longer under his control." She came forward and laid her hand on my shoulder. "Don't worry. Catalina will be thrilled to have you with her in Kansas City. Dario will adjust."

I tugged on my painted lip with my teeth. "Will Dante be in trouble?"

Mia nodded. "Don't worry about him. Dante is a grown man who's capable of making his own decisions."

My eyebrows knitted together. "He's a good man."

"Are you asking or telling?"

"Both. He's always been good to me."

"That's what matters. I've learned the men in the famiglia and those in the cartel aren't much different from one another, though they wouldn't admit to their similarities. There are good men and bad men on both sides. My brothers can both be good men. They are also both capable of doing bad things. It's not so much about separating the two identities as it is about loving both sides."

My cheeks rose. "You love Jano."

Pressing her lips together, Mia nodded. The tips of her lips curled upward. "You and Dante have an advantage over Jano and me—over Dario and Catalina. You two know one another. Not intimately...?" She let the word hang in the air.

I shook my head.

She sighed. "Good. I'm glad my brother didn't break that tradition."

"We've kissed."

"Aléjandro and I kissed before we were wed and while it was passionate" —she lifted her hands— "lightning didn't strike." She lowered her hands to her sides. "You two know each other and want to be married. That's why I'm helping you. I'm sick and tired of the men on both sides making decisions for women without their consent. I love Aléjandro now, but the night we wed, I never thought I would."

"I think I love Dante," I confessed. "Catalina said it was lust."

"There's nothing wrong with lust, Camila. Lust is a very important part of your relationship." She placed her hands on her stomach. "That twisty feeling down low that makes you squirm. The way your skin warms at the sight of the man you want beside you. And the tightness that beads your nipples when you know he's watching you."

I nodded. "That's the way Dante makes me feel."

"Rei?" she asked.

My smile faded. "No. I hate that this will hurt him, but I don't feel that way when I'm with him."

"There's no way to know how a marriage between the two of you would have worked. If I know Rei, he'll be understanding. Somewhere out there, there's a woman who will feel all those things for him. You lost your heart to Dante. That wasn't a conscious decision. Love shouldn't be ignored."

"I still can't believe that Dante wants me. He used to refer to me as a little girl."

"He wants you," she said. "If you ask me, the little girl comment was a way to remind himself that you were off-limits." She grinned. "By the way he was looking at you downstairs, he's no longer thinking of you as a little girl."

"And after our vows, I'll no longer be off-limits."

"Are you ready for that?"

Warmth filled my cheeks. "I think I am."

"Some sisterly advice?"

"Okay."

"You're not ready. That's not a bad thing." Mia scrunched her nose. "The first time isn't the best, but it gets much better."

"Your first time with Jano?"

Mia shook her head. "I was married before."

"Oh, I'm sorry. I forgot."

"Don't be sorry. I'd like to forget that marriage too." She scanned me up and down. "We need to get you downstairs so you can be a married woman by the stroke of midnight."

"At midnight, will our car turn into a pumpkin? Because I feel like I'm in a fairy tale."

"And Dante is Prince Charming." Mia went to the large bouquet of fresh flowers on a table in their suite and pulled an assortment from the vase. She trimmed the stems and wrapped them with a white ribbon. "Your bouquet." As she handed it to me, her eyes widened. "Oh, I have something blue for you."

"You do?"

She hurried into one of the closets. A few moments later, she returned with a garter. "It was mine, when I married Aléjandro. You can borrow it, and it will be your something borrowed and something blue."

I took a seat in one of the plush chairs. Slipping my foot out of one of the high-heeled shoes, I slid the garter up to my thigh. "My dress is old." I slipped my foot back into the shoe.

"My shoes you're wearing are new."

"Borrowed is definitely covered and now the garter is blue." I looked at the clock and saw that it was past 11:30. "I heard it is good luck to say your vows as the hands of the clock are rising."

"Then let me go downstairs and let them know the bride is ready."

As Mia left the bedroom suite, my phone buzzed.

Do I want to look?

Curiosity got the better of me as I lifted my phone and entered my passcode. The text message was from Catalina. I held my breath as I opened it.

. . .

"Em called me and told me what you're doing. Luckily, I was up with Ariadna, and Dario is asleep. I love you, but this will cause problems. Please think about the repercussions. If it's too late, you and Dante need to get to KS as quickly as possible. You'll be safer here."

I tossed my phone on the table with the remaining flowers. It wasn't too late to stop this. That didn't mean I wanted to. As Mia said, I'd lost my heart to Dante Luciano. It wasn't on purpose, but in the depth of my soul, I knew my heart was where it belonged. I could only hope that the consequences of our decision would quickly fade away.

Mia returned, pushing the door inward. "They're ready. Everyone is out by the pool." She looked down at the shoes. "Do you need help going down the stairs?"

"They're high, but I'm okay." I reached out and grabbed Mia's hand. "Thank you. I wish Catalina was here, but I'm glad I had a sister here to share this with me."

Her smile curled. "Dante is waiting."

SIXTEEN

Dante

S tanding outside near the pool gave me a sense of vulnerability. It was probably just the way I was raised in the bloody world of the Mafia. Nevertheless, it felt as if at any moment, we could be within someone's sights. I peered over the edge of the cliff down into the dark abyss. The salty scent lingering in the breeze and the crash of distant waves alerted me to the Pacific Ocean far below. I'd been here during the day and seen the glistening waves for myself.

High above, the dark sky above the sea twinkled with hundreds of stars, evidence that the earlier clouds had cleared.

"The bride-to-be is ready," Silas said, coming up behind me.

"You're sure it's safe out here?"

"I'm confident in my security system."

I jutted my chin toward the cliff. "Isn't that how the robbers got into this house before?"

"*Sí*. That was before the motion detectors and alarms were installed. I've increased the number of guards tonight."

"You did? When?"

"After *Señora* Roríguez informed me of the wedding."

The small hairs at the nape of my neck stood to attention. "Are you anticipating a problem?"

"I'm always anticipating a problem. It's my job. Jano and Mia are like my family to me. I wouldn't allow them to spend time out here if I wasn't confident they were secure."

I heard his sincerity and saw his determined expression. "They trust you. I will too. Don't let us down."

Silas nodded.

Aléjandro and Father Gallo joined me under the stars, the priest taking his spot beneath the archway of lights.

"*Señor* Luciano," he called me toward him.

I took my place standing to his left side. My dark jeans and t-shirt were hardly wedding apparel. Yet, here I was, with my back to the vast ocean and my eyes set on the inside of the house. Mia emerged, taking a seat next to her husband. I noticed with a hint of jealousy the casual way their fingers intertwined with one another's as if they couldn't be close without touching.

I'd lived my life as a bachelor, a loner. Seeing my sister and her husband and my brother and his wife were reminders of what I'd missed. The lights within the house went dark, leaving the only lighting out on the pool deck.

"Is everything—" I started to question, alarm spiking my already-tattered nerves.

Before I could get the rest of my sentence out, Camila stepped from the darkness in a long white dress, looking like an angel brought to earth. Her beauty took the wind from my lungs as her emerald gaze met mine. She smiled and walked forward. Fresh flowers were in her hand. Scanning from her long, luscious hair to the toes of her shoes, I thanked the Almighty that she chose me.

Of all the men in the world, Camila Ruiz chose a man who didn't deserve her—one who would spend his life trying to. No longer did I wonder why Dario hadn't chosen Camila. The reason was here and now. Coming from two completely different worlds, we never would have met. Dario's choice of Catalina brought Camila to me. She wasn't meant to be with Dario or even Reinaldo. Her fate was set the first time I laid eyes on her.

I lifted my hand, palm up. Camila reached for it, holding the flowers in the other hand. I closed my fingers around hers and turned toward the priest as the scent of cinnamon combined with the salty air.

The priest's voice penetrated my thoughts, bringing me to the present. "Camila Ruiz and Dante Luciano, have you come here to enter into marriage without coercion, freely and wholeheartedly?"

Looking down at her, I stared into her beautiful green eyes. "Yes," I replied.

"Yes," she said with a slight nod of her head.

"Are you prepared, as you follow the path of marriage, to love and honor each other as long as you both shall live?"

I squeezed her hand as we both answered affirmatively.

"Since it is your intention to enter into the covenant of Holy Matrimony, join your right hands and declare your consent before God and His Church."

Camila smiled as she looked down at our already-joined hands.

I followed the priest's prompts. "I, Dante Luciano, take you, Camila Ruiz, to be my wife. I promise to be faithful to you in good times and in bad, in sickness and in health, to love you and honor you all the days of my life."

Next, Camila repeated her vows, the words that would make her mine forever.

"I, Camila Ruiz, take you, Dante Luciano, to be my husband. I promise to be faithful to you in good times and in bad, in sickness and in health, to love you, honor you, and obey you all the days of my life."

I marveled at her strength and determination. No way had she imagined her wedding occurring in someone else's home as the clock neared midnight, without the comfort and support of her family surrounding her. Yet here she was, unwavering in her proclamation.

The priest spread his arms to his sides. "May the Lord in his kindness strengthen the consent you have declared before these witnesses and graciously bring to fulfillment his blessings within you. What God has joined, let no one put asunder." He grinned. "It is time for the giving and receiving of rings."

"Oh," Camila's eyes grew wide. "I don't have a ring."

"I have one."

We all turned to the unexpected voice. I stiffened, ready to reach for my gun.

"Em?" Camila said, her eyes filling with unshed tears as her hand began to tremble.

Emiliano came forward. "I hoped to get here in time to walk you down the aisle." He smiled at his sister. "I brought this." He extended his hand toward Camila. Lying on his palm was a gold band.

The tears my bride was holding back cascaded down her cheeks. "Em, that was *el abuelito's*. He gave it to you."

"And I'm giving it to you." He turned to me. "They're going to do everything they can to annul this marriage. Every irregularity will be scrutinized. Take the ring and complete the ceremony."

Twisting, I offered Em my right hand. "Thank you."

His lips quirked. "My warning still stands."

"I'll spend my life convincing her I deserve her."

"You don't."

I nodded. "I'm going to try."

Again, her brother offered the gold band to Camila. This time, she picked it up and turned back to Father Gallo. "I have a ring."

The priest looked at me.

"I have a ring, too."

"Then we should proceed. Dante."

I removed the ruby ring from my pocket and lifted Camila's left hand. "Camila, receive this ring as a sign of my love and fidelity. In the name of the Father, and the Son, and the Holy Spirit."

Camila's smile was radiant as she lifted my hand and pressed the band over my knuckle. "Dante, receive this ring as a sign..."

Her love.

Her fidelity.

They were mine and I'd treasure them as I would treasure her.

"In the sight of God and these witnesses, I now pronounce you husband and wife. Dante, you may now kiss your bride."

Leaning down, I cupped her cheek and brought my lips to hers, tasting her sweetness.

"Go in peace." As the priest's words came forth, a whirling sound came into range.

The noise grew louder as Silas yelled for everyone to go into the house. Seizing Camila's hand, I pulled her along with me as I unsheathed my gun. Silas closed the glass doors. With the lights within still off, our wedding party was covered in darkness as well as behind glass.

Each man was armed, the barrels of the guns reflecting the lights from outside.

"What is it?" Camila asked, her hand trembling in mine.

"Helicopter," Aléjandro answered. "Get back, away from the windows. Silas, contact the guards. Mia?"

"I'm here."

The whirling grew even louder, shaking the walls.

The whirl became deafening as if the helicopter were over the house.

Aléjandro shouted, "Take Camila, Viviana, and Father Gallo."

"Come this way," Mia instructed. Her silhouette barely showed against the backdrop of the front windows. Spotlights moved over the pool deck from above.

Fuck.

"Who did you tell?" I screamed over the noise at Emiliano.

"No one, motherfucker. I wouldn't risk my sister's life."

"Bring her here." Mia's voice called from the darkness.

"Where?" I asked.

"Safe room."

At the sound of the answer, Camila clung tighter to my hand and buried her face in my shirt. "No, please. I can't do this again." Her entire body trembled.

"Where is it?" I asked. Lowering my voice, I whispered in Camila's ear, "You'll be safe."

"I can't...I was alone."

"You won't be alone," I promised.

Mia directed me to Aléjandro's office. Within the closet, she moved a lever, causing the back bookcase to move. If there wasn't a threat to my family and those I cared about, I could be impressed.

My sister offered Camila her hand. "Come with me."

I'd take a thousand cuts from my enemies' weapons

over the terror in my new wife's eyes. When I find out who caused her this distress, I'll gut them, one by one.

"You're not alone," I reassured.

Rapid popping of gunshots came from outside the house causing Camila to jump.

"I can't leave you, Dante."

I kissed her hair. "You're not leaving me. I'm not leaving you. Be safe."

Father Gallo took her hand. Reluctantly, they both joined Mia in the safe room, followed by Viviana. Mia closed the bookcase. I turned off the closet light and closed the door. As I came around the corner, back into the living room, I saw the helicopter, hovering in the dark vastness beyond the pool.

"Fuck," Aléjandro roared.

Three men were in the helicopter. The side facing the house was open with a door gunner armed with an MP5 submachine gun. They were fucking close enough to make out their identities if their faces weren't obscured with ski masks. Bullets rained down over the pool deck, where we'd just been.

"The windows are bulletproof," Silas yelled as they quaked with the repeated impact of 800 rounds per minute, shredding the pool furniture, planters, and anything in their wake.

"Goddamn them," Aléjandro cursed.

We watched as the door gunner was struck, the bullet coming from the area to the side of the pool from the darkness. The helicopter wobbled. If not for his seatbelt, the damn door gunner would have fallen.

"Who the fuck are they?" I asked my brother-in-law.

"Border agents stopped a shipment of MP5s from coming into the US a few weeks ago."

"Yours?"

"They tried to link them to us. They belonged to Kozlov."

"Fucking Russians," I said through clenched teeth.

"Our guards don't have the firepower to bring down a chopper." As Silas spoke, the chopper turned to the darkness of the ocean and disappeared.

"This wasn't about the wedding?" I asked.

"I don't think so," Aléjandro answered. He turned to Silas. "Changing these windows saved our lives. Find out if any of our men were hit." He looked at me and Emiliano. "We'll get the all clear from the guards before we risk the women and collar."

I turned to the large clock. "Fuck, it's almost midnight." We had less than fifteen minutes. The hands were ticking upward.

Aléjandro went to a tablet on the kitchen counter and handed it to me. "Go, take this. Father Gallo will make your marriage legal." Next, he pulled his phone from his pocket. The conversation that ensued was not in English, yet I could tell it was upsetting him in the way the veins bulged in his neck and how his jaw tightened.

Holding the tablet, I waited.

Once he finished his conversation, he roared, a feral sound reverberating through the house.

"What else?" I asked.

"Rei's house in Sacramento was attacked tonight. Simultaneously. Timed to hit us both when we should be sleeping."

161

"That means this attack was against the cartel, not specifically our wedding."

Emiliano came to my side. "Is Rei all right?"

That was probably the question I should have asked.

Aléjandro's stare darkened, his pupils dilating. "Gerardo didn't have bulletproof glass. Rei is fine. He wasn't home. Two of our men on his patrol are dead."

CHAPTER
SEVENTEEN

Camila

The insulated walls deafened the whirl of the helicopter and blasts of gunshots. From inside the safe room, it was impossible to know what was happening outside. No way to know who was safe and who wasn't. It seemed unreal that once again I was hiding for my life.

Wedding day.

Wedding night.

We went from our ceremony to a safe room.

Not the wedding a little girl daydreams about.

The small room where we hid contained two twin beds, a desk, and chair. There was a small refrigerator stocked with water. And currently, it also contained four people. As Mia and I sat on one of the twin-sized beds with our backs against the wall, I pulled my knees to my chest and hugged my legs. Her hand lingered protectively over her midsection, a momma bear guarding the tiny life within. Looking around at the four walls, it was easy to determine that this room was a lot different than the sauna where I hid the last time a home was attacked.

The biggest difference was that I wasn't alone. Sitting across from Mia and me was Viviana. Father Gallo was seated on a straight-backed chair near the small desk.

Mia reached out, covering my hand with hers. "The men will be safe. Silas replaced all the windows with bulletproof glass."

Bulletproof glass.

Safe room.

"It hasn't even been a year since our house was attacked." I turned and looked at my new sister-in-law, seeing pity in her hazel stare. "Your house was attacked that same night."

Mia nodded. "We weren't home. This is the first time we've needed this room."

I took in the basic furnishings. "I don't want to live like this."

She grinned. "Dante's apartment is bigger."

"I mean in fear, fear that my husband will be hurt or worse. Fear that our privacy will be invaded. Fear of calls in the middle of the night."

Mia smiled a sad smile. "You just married the wrong man."

"I married the right man." Looking down, I saw the ruby ring and splayed my fingers. "This ring is beautiful."

Mia took my hand in hers. "It fits you. I thought it

would." She tilted her head. "You don't have to wear it forever. I'm sure Dante will buy you a big diamond once things settle down."

Twisting the band, I watched the way the red stone shone under the ceiling lights. "I don't want to get rid of it."

"Oh, that's not what I meant."

"Do you know where he got it?" I asked.

"Funny, it's like Em's story of the ring he brought you."

The mention of my brother's act of kindness and acceptance brought a grin to my lips.

Mia went on, "That ring belonged to our grandmother, Nonna Luna. She was our mother's mother."

I exhaled, appreciating Mia's story and wanting to learn more about Dante's family.

"Nonna Luna and Nonno Alessio were closer to Dante and me than to Dario. Dario had the attention of our father's parents. Even when my two brothers were young, Dario was the chosen one. The prince of the Lucianos." She turned my way. "Things haven't changed. There's no way that Andrés or Jorge would have changed their mind with Catalina as they did with you. No one would do that to the future capo."

"He's now capo."

"No longer a prince," Mia said. "He's the king. Our mother's parents gave Dante the attention he didn't receive from the Lucianos. I was born later and by that time, our father was capo. His father was gone. Our mother was dealing with the horrors of the man she married. Nonna and Nonno would take me for extended periods of time in the summer and on vacation with them."

I liked the way the story made Mia smile. "Did they do that for Dante?"

"I don't really know. He's older than I am. By the time they were taking me, he was a preteen. No vacations with grandparents. Father had the two boys to prepare for manhood."

I scrunched my nose. "I think that's kind of how it was for Em too. His childhood was cut shorter than Cat's and mine."

"Dante knew from an early age that his job was to protect Dario at all costs. Our father thought if he made them tough, they would either survive or kill one another."

"What?" My eyes widened.

"The good news is that Dario and Dante didn't take the second option. Instead, they joined forces against our father." Mia scoffed. "I wish I could have witnessed the moment the great Vincent Luciano realized he'd raised two killers, and the man they hated most was their own father."

"That's a shame," Viviana said.

Up until that moment, I hadn't thought about being overheard.

Viviana went on, "Jorge raised Jano and Rei to be resilient without making them hate one another or him."

"How did they do that?" Mia asked.

Viviana smiled. "Josefina." She nodded toward Mia's stomach. "It is what you'll do too. Josefina loves unconditionally. That love is so overpowering that hate can't survive. She loves her husband and her children."

Mia's nostrils flared as she nodded. "My mother and father had a difficult marriage."

"Children, even babies, sense the emotions of others." Viviana smiled. "You love Jano. You care about the women at the school. Mia, you have a good heart. Your *bebé* will learn his or her role in the world and also know love."

A tear glistened on my sister-in-law's cheek until she casually wiped it away.

"It's true," I added. "You helped me marry Dante. You didn't have to do all you did."

"Well, the next wedding we host, I'd like to avoid the helicopter and gunfire."

Father Gallo looked at his watch. "I hope we can get the online license worked out soon."

"Oh," I said, "does that mean we're not married?"

"You're married in the eyes of our Lord, Mrs. Luciano."

"Mrs. Luciano," I repeated softly.

"That's you," Mia said.

The eyes of the Lord might satisfy my mother, but it wouldn't my father.

We all turned to the opening of the door.

The air in the room electrified, crackling with the power of the men entering, the scent of sulfur and gunpowder preceding them.

Aléjandro entered first, going directly to his wife and pulling her into his arms. It was the second man, the one with the laser-focused dark stare who had my attention. "Is everyone safe?" I asked.

"One guard was injured," Em said, entering last. Standing tall, he crossed his arms in front of him. "Rei's house was hit at the same time. This attack wasn't about the wedding. It was against the Roríguez cartel."

"Is Rei all right?" Mia asked.

Jano replied, "He lost two guards, and his house sustained more damage, but he's okay."

Father Gallo stood. "Mr. Luciano, we should secure your marriage license."

Dante reached for me, his large hand open. My focus went to the gold band on the fourth finger of his left hand. Without pause, I laid my hand in his. As his fingers closed, I stood. The high heels from the ceremony were taken off as we entered the safe room, leaving me four inches shorter than I was during our wedding and bringing my cheek to my husband's chest.

Dante wrapped his arms around me, pulling me to him. Beneath his shirt, his heart beat at a steady rate. Peering upward, I looked through my lashes. "I was scared."

"You were safe."

"I wasn't afraid for me. I was worried about all of you."

"Silas saved the night," Jano said. "Let's get out of this small room."

He was right in his description. The room was small before. Add three giant men and the room was miniscule.

With my hand in Dante's, he led me into the living room, everyone else following. Within seconds, Dante and Father Gallo were online, navigating the wedding license. Standing against the wall, I watched as the two men impatiently entered the necessary data. Silas and Jano took Mia out onto the deck, showing her the carnage. With the glass doors open, the night was eerily quiet. A slight breeze gave me a chill as the three of them inspected what was left of their outdoor furniture. Thankfully, the damage was to material things, not people. Mia was shaking her head as Jano comforted her.

"Camila," Dante called, pulling me from being a voyeur.

Barefooted, I went toward him.

"You're my wife, and I have so much to learn about you."

Warmth filled my cheeks. "And a lifetime to do that."

"Currently," Father Gallo said, "we need your help with personal information."

My mind had gone to other places. "What do you need to know?"

For the next five minutes, the three of us sat at Mia's kitchen bar and entered numbers. Birth dates, Social Security numbers, driver's license numbers... the list went on and on. I'd married a man whose middle name I didn't know. It was probably all right. Dante didn't know mine either.

Aurelio.

Dante Aurelio Luciano.

Isabella.

Camila Isabella Ruiz.

Camila Isabella Luciano.

The site then required a live video of the two of us, verifying that we were together and both in agreement.

Dante pulled me between his spread legs. His head cleared mine as we both stared into the camera at the top of the small screen.

"Our first wedding picture."

"No, it's not," Viviana said. "I took pictures during the ceremony."

My cheeks rose. "Thank you."

"The next question," Father Gallo said, "asks if you want to keep your maiden name or take your husband's."

I turned in his embrace, facing the man who was now my husband. "Would you have a problem with me keeping my maiden name?"

He tilted his forehead to mine and lowered his tone in a way that made my insides twist. "Yes. You're now and forever Camila Luciano."

"I like the way that sounds." I turned back to the priest. "It sounds like I'm changing my name."

"Tell me you won't give in to him so easily on all matters of importance."

"Here's a secret. I didn't give in." I found Dante's hand and intertwined our fingers. "I want his name. I want the world to know that he's my husband and I'm his wife."

Father Gallo smiled. "Son, I think you have a good one here."

"The best," Dante replied.

"That does it," the priest said with a smile. "You're officially married in the eyes of our Lord and the State of California." He bowed his head and looked up. "Congratulations, Mr. and Mrs. Luciano." He stood. "Now, after all that excitement, if it's safe, I will be leaving."

We turned to Silas, who was back inside with Jano, Mia, and Em.

"Our guards have completed a sweep of the property," Silas said. "You're safe to leave; however, the cars on the driveway are totaled."

"Your rental car," I said to Dante.

"I don't give a fuck about the rental car." He turned to Father Gallo. "I'll replace your car, Father."

"That would be very kind of you."

"Tomorrow, you'll have a new one."

"New isn't necessary."

"New," Jano said, entering the conversation. "Tonight, Silas will drive you back to the rectory."

"Thank you for an eventful evening."

Dante looked over at the large clock. "It's officially a new day. In the morning, we will need to let your father know that you won't be available for your engagement party."

"Are we leaving now for Kansas City?" I asked.

"You're staying here for the night," Jano said. "Viviana has prepared the primary suite. Mia and I will sleep in the guest room."

"You don't need—"

Jano lifted his hand. "We need some traditions to be honored."

"Jano," Em said with a phone to his ear. "Rei is on the phone." He tilted his head toward Jano's office.

Dante stood. "I'm here to help."

Em lowered the phone. "I never expected this

sentence to come out of my mouth, but tonight, you're needed in consummating your marriage. All hell is going to break loose tomorrow. Don't give them any reason to undo what was done tonight."

My cheeks grew hotter with each of my brother's instructions. It wasn't quite like the chants of 'bed her' that Dante tried to shout at Dario and Catalina's wedding, but the outcome would be the same.

Sirens blared in the distance.

"Go," Em said, "Aléjandro will satisfy the police. No one will disturb you."

Dante offered me his hand. "Mrs. Luciano, you heard your brother."

As we started to walk away, I stopped. "Wait, are the upstairs windows also bulletproof?"

"Yes," Jano replied. He lifted his eyebrows. "The room isn't soundproof."

I clung to Dante's arm as we walked together toward the primary suite.

CHAPTER
EIGHTEEN

Camila

My mind spun with each step up the staircase. The memories of the last twelve hours swirled with hurricane-strength emotions. It seemed impossible that Papá had called me into his office this very afternoon. No, it's officially tomorrow. He called me to his office yesterday.

In the hours following that meeting my whole world changed.

Our whole world.

The disappointment at my father's decision and his unwillingness to listen sent me reeling. It wasn't until I saw Dante and knew he'd come across the country to fight for me that I regained my footing. If he could fight for me—for us, so could I.

Dante's and my marriage was the throwing of a

stone into a lake. The ripples would flow in every direction, having repercussions beyond the two of us.

A quick look up at the man holding my hand was all the reassurance I needed to know I'd made my own decision. Dante was the man I wanted, and by the warmth of his body next to mine, he wanted me too.

Neither of us said a word as we ascended the staircase, leaving those below behind who knew exactly what was about to happen. My brother even mandated it. Nothing made sense and yet everything was as it should be.

Dante opened the door to the primary suite, and we walked inside.

I took in the room, the closed French doors leading to a balcony overlooking the pool and ocean. There was a comfortable area with a loveseat, chair, and small table. The main focus of the room, situated near the balcony doors, was the large king-sized bed.

"Do you think it's a little weird to be in Jano and Mia's bedroom?"

Dante scoffed. "Traditions. Aléjandro and Mia were in your parents' bedroom."

I scrunched my nose. "Okay. I'd rather be here than in my parents' bedroom. That would be..." I couldn't come up with the best word. If instead of words, I could have used emojis, it would be the one with the face vomiting.

Dante closed the door, turning the lock in the doorknob.

"You think that will keep them out?"

"My gun will keep them out. As surprising as it is,

174

everyone downstairs is on our side. We are where they want us."

I made my way to the balcony doors. With my hands on the handles, I asked, "Is it safe to open these?"

Dante came behind me, the warmth of his front covered my back. He placed his hand over mine and turned the handle. Immediately, the sound of the surf below filled our ears. There wasn't any furniture out on the balcony. A quick look below and we saw Viviana picking up pieces of the furniture that remained in tatters on the pool deck.

As we stepped out onto the cool concrete balcony, strands of my hair blew around my face. "Do you think there used to be chairs out here?"

"Before they were shot all to hell?" Dante said. "I would guess." He reached for my hand. "Is there any way I can make you forget, if only for a while, about what happened with the helicopter?"

Taking a deep breath, I lifted my chin to catch his gaze. "I don't know," I replied honestly. "I know I'd like for you to try."

Dante ran his hands down both of my arms, a ghost of a touch that sent shock waves through my nervous system. His head tilted, fire burning in his gaze as he secured a strand of long hair behind my ear. "If I haven't told you, you're gorgeous, Camila. When you appeared out of the darkness in this white dress, I couldn't believe that you were willingly coming to me, to marry me, and to be my wife. You looked too heavenly to be real."

I lifted my hand to his cheek, feeling the coarseness of his day's beard growth. "I think I fell in love with you

175

during my first visit to Kansas City. Do you remember helping me see Emerald Club? Catalina was against it, and Dario was..."

"Dario."

"Yes," I said with a grin. "You thought I was older than I was."

"Because," he said, backing me against the wall to the side of the balcony, "I was attracted to you the first time I saw you—the night before Dario's wedding. Then I found out you were too young, too sweet, and too innocent for me."

"Too bad."

Dante's lips quirked. "You're not bad."

Keeping my chin raised, I found myself lost in his dark stare. "No, I'm saying *too bad*. If you think I'm wrong for you, it's too late. We're married. It's official, according to Father Gallo, in the eyes of the Lord and in the eyes of California." I wiggled my ring finger. "I'm a married woman."

"There's a stigma in my world, our world. I probably learned it from my father. Love makes you weak. Success is all about power." His Adam's apple bobbed. "I've seen that isn't accurate with Dario and Catalina. I can't say I loved you the first time I saw you. I can say I lusted after you." Pressing his hips toward mine, I felt the pressure of his confined erection. "I thought I loved you when I proposed, but when Dario informed me that you were no longer to be mine, I felt that love deep into my bones. It's fierce and strong, Camila. I love you. I will spend forever hoping you feel that because you're now mine."

As I reeled from his declaration, Dante pressed his

strong lips together and tilted his handsome face. Slowly he trailed the pad of his finger down my cheek, my neck, and my collarbone. His touch was like the striking of a match, methodically setting my flesh ablaze. His dark stare intensely followed his finger as it lowered down my chest and to the apex of the sundress's neckline. After lingering long enough to make my nipples harden, Dante's gaze came back to mine. "And now it's time to make you forget."

His deep baritone warning sent shivers down my spine and left goose bumps in their wake. I could ask what he wanted me to forget, but I was done talking. I'd made my decision.

It wasn't that I would have denied him sex before we were legally wed. By the way my body reacted to his mere presence, I would have acquiesced. However, he never asked. That didn't make me feel rejected in any way. On the contrary, his patience made me feel respected.

Marriage—or lack thereof—was no longer a barrier to sex. We'd said our vows, signed our license. I was ready to learn what other women knew, the feeling of a man touching her, teasing her, loving her, and being inside her.

I read books and watched movies.

Now, I wanted to learn for myself, to experience what I'd only imagined. I wanted to be the heroine in my own story with the hero of my choosing.

Dante's lips took mine—strong and possessive. He wasn't staking his claim. That he'd already done. Dante was declaring me for himself. I was his, the deal signed, the ring in place. My hands climbed his broad shoulders higher to his thick neck, and up to his wavy dark mane. I took in his scent of leather, spice, and enough gunpowder to add the hint of danger.

His kiss consumed me, twisting my core. As his tongue sought entrance, my body tightened, painfully so, as synapse after synapse exploded within me. Heat accompanied the detonations, threatening to engulf the two of us in a fiery inferno.

I gasped for breath as his kisses lowered, following the trail his finger had explored. A moan escaped my lips as he peppered my skin, slowly and meticulously, and his lips moved down my body. I jumped at the sight of Dante's knife.

"What?"

"We have our traditions, too."

A long-ago memory of Mia telling Cat about the cutting of the wedding dress came back. I stood perfectly still, willing myself not to move as my husband sliced one spaghetti strap like butter and then the other. The neckline lowered, revealing my breasts. Lifting my chin, my neck arched as the combination of sea air and his warm breath caused my hardened nipples to turn to diamonds.

"You're fucking perfect."

A man like Dante had probably been with many women more experienced and definitely shapelier. "They're small."

He sucked one nipple into his mouth. I squealed as he nipped my flesh with his teeth. "Perfect," he said against my skin. "I won't hear any other description."

Taking a step back, Dante stared down at me, my dress now resting at my waist, below my exposed breasts. "Look at you, with your hair tousled, your skin marred by my attention." He brought his finger again to my neck. "Your artery is pulsating, and your breathing is erratic." His lips quirked. "Your scent is divine. I can smell your arousal just as I did that night in my apartment."

Warmth filled my cheeks at his accurate description.

He ran his palm over his cheek. "I should shave. Your skin is sensitive to my scruff."

I shook my head. "I like it."

In one fell swoop, Dante lifted me from the concrete balcony. I wrapped my arms around his neck as he carried me back into the bedroom. Gently setting my feet back on the floor, he closed the doors to the balcony and took a step back. "I want to see you, Camila. All of you."

The goose bumps were back.

When I didn't move, he leaned closer, whispering a menacing murmur and coating my ear and neck with his warm breath. "All of you."

Nodding, I pushed down my sundress, the material pooling around my feet.

His brown orbs burned with unspoken desire.

Even a woman as inexperienced as I noticed the strain of his erection against his dark jeans.

Dante lifted my chin. "When we're alone, I want you to remember that you belong to me. You're mine to do with as I want. Outside our private bubble, I love your fire and determination. You're incredibly sexy standing up for yourself. In private, I want to hear your desires as long as you remember that I'm in charge."

I swallowed, my mouth suddenly dry.

"Can you remember that?"

My nostrils flared as I nodded, my chin still in his grasp.

"Now, what did I say I wanted to see?"

"All of me." My voice came out stronger than I anticipated. I straightened my neck. "I want to see you, too. I've never seen..."

Releasing my chin, Dante's cheeks rose as his smile curled. "Oh, beautiful, you will see me. First, it's my turn. Don't make me repeat myself again."

Catching the waistband of my panties with my fingers, I pulled them down, keenly aware that they were wet with the arousal he'd claimed to know was there. I let the lacy material drop to the carpet and join the puddle of my dress.

Something resembling a primitive growl echoed through the bedroom suite as Dante stepped back and slowly walked around me. His intense focus returned the scorching flames to my exposed skin. All my skin. One. Two. Three circles, each one weakening my resolve and my knees.

CHAPTER

NINETEEN

Dante

Mine.

It was the one word running on repeat as I scanned every inch of Camila's sensual being. She was as I said, fucking perfect. "I want to explore every peak." I lowered my lips and sucked one of her nipples. Her shriek was a lightning bolt to my hardened cock. "Every valley." My lips teased the flesh between her breasts. "Until I've solved every mystery of your body."

Camila wobbled as if she was hypnotized by the sound of my voice.

As I'd done on the balcony, I lifted her naked body to my chest and carried her to the bed. Throwing back the blankets, I laid her on the black satin sheets.

Black.

Camila's innocence would be evident after I took her, but it wouldn't be the stark broadcast of red on a crisp white canvas. Grabbing the back of my shirt, I pulled it over my head, tossing it onto the floor. I made quick work of my holsters, removing my gun and two knives. By the time I was down to my boxer briefs, Camila was sitting up, her body up to her breasts covered with a sheet, staring in my direction with the sexiest smirk I'd ever seen.

"You were saying, about your experience with seeing men?"

"We have a pool. I've seen what you're showing me."

"You've seen it. Have you touched it?"

Camila shook her head.

I crooked my finger and bid her to come to me.

There was a millisecond of a delay. Yet before I could say a word, Camila threw back the sheet revealing her perfect body, and getting off the bed, came toward me. Reaching for her hand, I brought it to my chest.

Camila splayed her fingers. "I feel your heart beating." She ran her finger over a scar on my pectoral region and more on my biceps. Her smile dimmed. "You have so many scars."

"Badges of honor, my father used to say. Each one proves I survived."

Camila shook her head. "Will you tell me about them?"

"I don't remember all the stories. They blend together."

With both her hands against my shoulders, she

leaned closer. Her softness against my hardness caused my cock to twitch and my balls to draw up.

"May I see all of you?" she asked.

"If I pull myself out, this is going to go a lot faster than I want it to. You will do more than see, but first, I want to learn those mysteries."

Her grin grew. "What mysteries?"

Taking her hand, I led her back to the bed and lay down at her side, my head supported by my hand, my elbow on the pillow. I stared down into her green velvet stare. "Mysteries." I bent my neck closer and blew a warm breath behind her ear, causing her to giggle as her flesh prickled with goose bumps. "You're ticklish behind your ear."

I continued my exploration, kissing and nipping. Her nipples were ultrasensitive, beading with the slightest attention. This time I moved lower, kisses and nips down her flat stomach, over her protruding hips. The sweet aroma of her essences beckoned me lower as she wiggled beneath my touch.

"Dante." My name hung in the air.

"I'm still solving mysteries."

She pressed her legs together. Lifting my head, I met her gaze. "Mine."

"It's just..." She shook her head. "Are you going to...?"

My smile grew. "I'm going to explore your sweet, wet pussy."

"Oh God. Like with your mouth? Do people really do that?"

I couldn't hold back my laugh. "Yes, beautiful. People really do that, and more than do it, they like it."

"Maybe we should shower first."

"No fucking way. I'm already addicted to your scent, and I haven't gotten my first lick."

She flung her arm over her eyes. "I'm embarrassed."

"Fuck no." I climbed up her body until our noses met. "Never. Remember the night you came to my apartment?"

Camila nodded.

"The night you orgasmed against me?"

"Yes, I remember."

"You were so wet, you left a spot of your come on my shorts."

Her eyes opened wider. "I didn't."

"You did. I fucking jacked off to the smell of those shorts for weeks. Now, I want to taste it." Before she could argue or her cheeks could become pinker, I lifted her over me. She straddled my torso with her petite hands on my shoulders and her luscious tits in my face.

"Dante, what...?"

"Do it again."

"Do what?"

"Rub yourself on me. Let me watch you."

Camila's upper lip disappeared behind her teeth.

Scooting up toward the headboard, I lowered her to my lap with her legs bent near my waist. "I'm rock-hard for you, but I want you loosened up, relaxed, and ready." I flexed my hips, pushing my hardness against her cunt.

"I don't..."

She lifted her hands back to my shoulders. Closing her eyes, she moved, her torso tightening and swaying as she rubbed her pussy over my cock. Back and forth. I studied her expressions, sensing when she felt pleasure. She was a work of art to behold. An erotic play written and directed to fulfill not only the desires of the actors but also the audience. By the time the final curtain fell, there would be multiple climaxes.

Her eyes opened as my hands came to her round ass. "Keep going."

As her movements quickened, I parted her folds, my finger submerging in her soaked, tight, soft pussy. She mewed as her forehead fell to my shoulder, still moving in a rhythm of her own creation. While I missed the sight of her beautiful face, I craved the feel of her body against mine. Each ministration pushed her breasts against my chest as a second finger joined the first.

She was so tight.

Camila's breaths came faster as her speed increased.

"Hold on to the headboard," I instructed.

"What...?"

I slid down until my head was on the pillow. Camila's thighs were on either side of my face, and her dripping pussy was over my mouth. The first lick sent her into a spiral as her body convulsed. I reached for her hands and directed them to the solid wood headboard.

She held on tight as I feasted on the delicacy before me. I held her hips as she bucked. It was as I nipped her clit that Camila screamed, the bedroom echoing with her sounds of pleasure.

All at once, I flipped her. Camila was light as a feather. Positioning and repositioning her was as easy as turning myself. She leaned her head to the side, granting me access to her sensitive, soft neck as I pressed my body over hers. More than a little satiated, her bent knees relaxed, flopping to the sides. If I didn't have on my boxer briefs, I'd be inside her.

My lips found hers as I devoured her mouth as I had her cunt. Camila didn't back away from her own taste; she kissed back, ravenous for what I had to offer. I kissed her neck and collarbone as I freed my erection from the confines of the boxer briefs.

Stilling, I waited for Camila's eyes to open. Once the green was before me, I asked, "Are you on the pill?"

She blinked. "What? No. My mother wouldn't...Do you want me to be?"

A smile lifted my cheeks. "Probably not the perfect timing for this discussion, but you want to continue classes, right?"

As she contemplated her answer, I directed the tip of my cock to her folds.

Camila's eyes opened wide.

"I'm trying to distract you, beautiful. We'll deal with birth control another day."

Pressing her lips together, she nodded.

"Look at me."

The satiation haze disappeared as she stared into my eyes.

"I want to make this good."

With her hands on my shoulders, she shrugged. "Cat and Mia both say it gets better."

"How was the oral?" I asked, further distracting as I pressed into her.

"Better than I..." She bit her upper lip.

She's like a fucking glove three sizes too small.

"Oh." Her long lashes flutter. "It was...well, I came."

I pressed further.

Camila palmed my cheeks. "Do it. I'm as ready as I'll be."

Lowering my forehead to hers, I watched her eyes, the tightness in her jaw, and the tight muscles along her temples. With a deep inhale, I pushed through the barrier she saved for me. My inspection of her face continued. "I won't move."

Camila's lips curled and her green eyes glistened with unshed tears. "Move." She wiggled beneath me. "I feel so full." Her expression changed. "Is that how it should feel?"

"I haven't been on the other side, but yeah."

Slowly, I pulled out only to press in again. As I created a rhythm, Camila's tenseness subsided, and she began rocking with me. Although I intended to stay slow and gentle, the grip of her pussy on my cock was earth-quaking. A few more thrusts and I sensed my balls tightening.

Reaching down, I found her clit and rubbed circles until her moans filled my ears. As her canal quivered, a deep guttural roar escaped my lips, and my cock throbbed in its tight new home.

Again, I dropped my forehead to hers and peppered her cheeks and lips with kisses. "Are you all right?"

Camila's smile beamed beneath me. "It was better than I expected."

Rolling, I broke our connection. "Remember, it gets better."

She sat up, looking down at her legs. "Is there... there's blood."

"There is, but it's not as glaring on these black sheets." I got up from the bed. In the bathroom, my cock glistened with the mixture of our come and her blood. A primal, feral sense of duty, sacrifice, and protection built within me. The whole virgin thing was never a deciding factor in choosing a wife. That was until now.

Camila was mine.

Only mine.

That knowledge unleashed an overpowering sense within me to take care of Camila and spend my life fulfilling her every need. As I carried a washcloth to the bed to tend to her physical necessities, the world around our bubble came back with a vengeance.

Tonight, I'd sleep with my wife.

Tomorrow we'd face the world as a married couple.

CHAPTER
TWENTY

Camila

My eyelids fluttered as consciousness awakened my senses. Warmth. I opened my eyes to the source of that heat, the man lying at my side. My smile faded as I moved, uncomfortably aware of the tenderness of my legs and between my legs. Memories came back as I snuggled beneath the blankets wondering how late we'd slept.

Dante rolled in my direction. His tousled dark hair reminded me of the number of times I'd woven my fingers through his locks. I studied his high cheekbones and protruding brow, and the way his long lashes fanned below his eyes. This handsome, dangerous, and powerful man was my husband.

Before I could reach out, his dark eyes opened; their

focus settled on me as his lips curled. "Good morning, Mrs. Luciano."

"Good morning, my husband." I pulled my left hand out from the warmth of the covers and looked at the stunning ruby ring. "Mia told me that this ring belonged to your grandma."

Dante turned to his back and inspected the ring on his left hand. "And this one belonged to your grandfather." He looked in my direction. "Tell me what kind of ring you want. When we get back to Kansas City, I'll take you to the best jewelry store."

"I want this ring. Unless...does Mia want it back?"

"Mia offered it to me for you. No strings attached." His smile grew. "But seriously, you're my wife. In case you haven't heard, the Luciano men are loaded. Don't you want an obscenely giant diamond?"

"I believe the Hope Diamond is locked away at the Smithsonian."

Dante reached for my hands. "You're thinking too small. The Hope Diamond is only forty-five and a half carats. The Cullinan Diamond is over 3,000 carats."

A giggle escaped my lips. "I've never heard of the Cullinan Diamond. Where is it?"

"Tower of London." He shook his head. "Not to worry. The famiglia has some of the best thieves in the business. Say the word. I'll give the order, and the diamond will be yours."

"The famiglia has the best thieves?"

"Yes," he said, pulling me closer. "We now have you."

The keycard I'd stolen from Contessa and pickpocketed from Dante.

I scooted closer, suddenly aware of my nakedness.

Watching my expression, Dante's smile faded. "Are you sore?"

"A little."

"So, morning sex...?"

"As I recall, you said in this bubble, you're in charge."

"I am, but I'm not a monster or at least not in this bubble. Pressing my cock into your tight pussy was a kind of heaven I want to keep enjoying. If that means letting you heal, I can do it."

"When are we going to Kansas City?"

"Dario told me to return within twenty-four hours." He lifted his wrist and looked at his watch. "That means we should clean up." As he inhaled, his nostrils flared. "And go to your house. We need to talk to your father."

I shook my head. "No. If I go back, they'll want me to stay. What time is it?"

"Almost seven." He kissed my nose. "Yesterday was a long day."

"Can we have a few more minutes in our bubble?"

"How about we shower and then I call Dario?"

That reminded me. "Cat knows about us—the wedding. She talked to Em."

"Oh fuck. I should probably call him sooner rather than later." He reached for his phone. "Shit, I have missed calls."

Tugging at the sheet, I wrapped it around my body and stood.

"What's with the dark Roman goddess attire?" Dante asked, standing in his naked Greek-god beauty. My focus went to the part of his body I'd never before seen. Oh, I felt it, but now it was right there.

Dante laughed. "I told you you'd see all of me."

I shook my head. "How did that fit inside me?"

"Perfectly."

"And it gets bigger?" I moved my gaze to his. Amusement glistened in his dark orbs.

"It's about to show you if you keep looking at it like that. What's with the sheet?" he asked again.

"I'm not wearing any clothes."

He came closer and tugged at the sheet. "I like you without clothes." He pulled the sheet away, letting it drop to the floor. "I'm considering implementing a new rule in our apartment. As long as we don't have company, the entire apartment will be a clothes-free zone."

"It gets cold in Missouri."

"That's what I'm for."

I looked up at his chiseled jaw now covered with more beard growth. "Were you serious about birth control last night?"

"That's what you remember about last night?"

"I remember many things about last night, but that's one."

"Yes, I'm serious."

"Just like that? Catalina and Dario have Ariadna, and Jano and Mia are pregnant."

"Thus, the need for birth control," he said. "Abstinence is off the table."

I tilted my head to the side. "You don't want children?"

Exhaling, Dante sat on the edge of the bed and pulled me to his lap. With his penis making its presence known, I peered down and up.

"Ignore it."

"That's kind of hard," I said with a giggle.

"Yeah, you make it that way." He teased my hair away from my face. "There will be a lot of these subjects, things we should have talked about before our wedding. We're going to need to tackle them one at a time. My guess is that we'll have enough friction from the outside, especially at first. You and I can handle whatever comes our way as long as we talk about it."

"Children?" I again asked, unsure how I felt about the subject. Honestly, it was never a question of *if* in my upbringing, but *when*. When was after marriage.

I was married.

He replied, "Yes, probably."

"Probably?" I questioned.

Dante inhaled, his chest inflating before he exhaled. "Listen, I'm not against children. You're young. We have time to discuss it." He furrowed his brow. "This is a shitty world. What happened here last night and to you months ago are reasons to wait. And then there's your classes. Your father made it clear during our negotiations that you finishing school was a priority."

I nodded. "I want to finish my degree." I palmed his cheeks, relishing the roughness of his beard and briefly imagining that roughness at my core. I tried to focus on the topic at hand before my nipples beaded and gave away my desires. "As for the world, you're right. It can be shitty, but we can't make our decisions based on that."

"When we get home, we'll make you an appointment with Catalina's doctor. Until then, I'll do a better job of pulling out."

"Someday?"

"Someday."

"Probably or definitely?"

"Do you always get your way?" he asked with a grin.

"I don't know. Will I?"

Dante nodded. After kissing my forehead, he stood, lowering my feet to the floor. "I'd like to join you in the shower, but I better touch base with Dario. You can go ahead without me."

I started to walk toward the bathroom and stopped. "Dante, I know we'll do what Dario wants you to do. But if we go to my house, promise me that you won't leave me there."

He slapped his fist against his chest. "You have my sworn promise."

Swallowing, I nodded. "I trust you."

About ten minutes later, as I stepped from the shower and wrapped myself in a towel, the bathroom door opened. No longer naked, Dante was wearing his boxer briefs. His expression did little to mask the fact that since waking, he had a change in his demeanor.

"Dario was happy for us?"

He shook his head. "I wouldn't use that description. He and Catalina are on their way here."

"What? Why?"

"Jorge Roríguez is on his way from Mexico."

I staggered and reached for the vanity. "Because of us?"

"Us and the attack last night."

"Jorge knows," I said, thinking aloud. "Does that mean my father knows?"

Dante nodded. "It seems that as we slept, the entirety of the famiglia and Roríguez cartel were brought up to speed."

"Have you talked to anyone downstairs?"

"I'm going to hurry and shower and go down."

"Okay. I'll be down as soon as I dry my hair and get dressed."

It seemed surreal that I was drying my hair and wearing a towel as Dante showered nude in the same bathroom. That was what married people did. I assumed that was what they did. As I applied a little of the makeup Mia offered me last night, some blush and mascara, the concerns about my father settled in my chest, taking root deep in my soul.

Tears filled my eyes as I imagined being separated from Dante.

By the time he got out of the shower, my eye makeup was ruined. I splashed water on my face and hurried from the bathroom.

"What the fuck?" Dante followed me, his muscular body dotted with water and wearing a towel around his waist. He seized my shoulders. "Are you crying?"

"I didn't want you to see."

"Camila, what happened?"

"I'm afraid Papá and *el Patrón* will say our marriage isn't legal or something. I'm afraid they'll make me stay in California." More tears slid down my cheeks. "I want to be your wife."

He pulled me against his damp chest and surrounded me with his arms. "I told Dario we were legally married by a priest."

I blinked away the tears. "What did he say?"

"Fuck was a repeated word, but in between the fucks, he said he'd do what he could to help us."

That gave me hope. "He said he'd help?"

"Stop worrying. I will not leave you behind with your family."

"Or with Rei?"

"Fuck no. Not a chance."

After a soft kiss, Dante stepped into his boxer briefs and put on the dark jeans he'd worn yesterday.

As he dressed, I realized my clothing dilemma. "I only have my sundress or the shorts, tank top, and sweatshirt I wore away from the house. And my dress... traditions..."

"Put on the shorts and we'll ask Mia to help. I'm sure she has something you can wear."

"I really don't want to face *el Patrón* in short shorts and a hoodie sweatshirt."

Once I had on the shorts, tank top, and hoodie, Dante headed downstairs, and I pulled my hair back into a low ponytail. It was as I was leaving the bathroom again that the bedroom door opened.

Mia entered. "Dante told me to come in. Are you okay?"

"I'm scared to death about what is going to happen today." I reached for my own hands to keep them from trembling. "*El Patrón* is on his way."

Mia nodded. "He's upset about the attacks on Rei's and our house."

"So, this isn't about Dante and me?"

She reached for my hand and led me to the sofa near the windows. "Aléjandro spoke to Rei last night about everything. He said Rei took the news well. He was disappointed, but Aléjandro explained that you and Dante have a history."

"Dante said Dario is upset."

Mia pressed her lips together and shook her head. "He's permanently upset. The only time he isn't is with Catalina." She patted my knee. "And Dante said she's with him. That's a good thing. This morning, Valentina discovered you were gone. Your bodyguard didn't know that you'd left."

I scrunched my nose. "Poor Miguel. It's not his fault."

"Emiliano told them what happened."

My stomach twisted. "I should call my mother."

"Probably, but I think they're on their way. According to Aléjandro, Andrés called Jorge, furious. He wants the alliance broken. That's why Dario is on his way too." She inhaled and exhaled. "We knew there would be issues."

"Issues. The cartel boss and famiglia capo dei capi are both coming here—that's more than an issue." I nibbled on my lip. "Can they make us unmarry?"

"I want to tell you no and not to worry."

"You want to?" I asked.

"They made me marry. They made Catalina marry. They can probably annul your marriage." Before I could respond, Mia went on, "You and Dante must convince them otherwise. Catalina and I are on your side."

"Have you spoken to her?"

"No, but if I know your sister, she'll stand by you. She's most likely the reason that Dario hasn't completely lost his shit."

I looked down, seeing my bare legs and the shorts. "Last night" —warmth filled my cheeks— "Dante cut the straps of my sundress."

Mia's smile bloomed. "Savage Italian traditions. Isn't that what you called them?"

I had.

"It was only the straps, and it was kind of sexy." I looked around. "But that means I only have this to wear."

Mia stood and looked down at me. "Nope. That won't do for the audience you're about to receive. I'm probably two or three sizes bigger than you even when I'm not pregnant. But Viviana is closer to your size."

"Do you think she has anything I could wear?"

"Since I convinced her to do away with the maid uniforms, she's expanded her wardrobe. Let me ask her, and we'll work out something."

I stood. "Thank you. I keep saying that, but I mean it. Thank you for standing by us."

"I never had a sister, and now I have two. They just happen to also be sisters. It's very complicated." She squeezed my hand. "But the best things always are."

Thirty minutes later, I was dressed in a long orange skirt with a white short-sleeved top. Mia came up with some chunky necklaces, and I decided my tennis shoes were perfectly acceptable. I added some curls to my hair on each side of my face and styled my ponytail neater. As I took one last look in the mirror, I noticed the ruby ring.

Holding my left hand against my chest, I remembered Dante's promise.

Tonight, I would be with my husband, wherever we were. We'd be together.

"Camila."

I peeked out of the bathroom to see Dante.

He stopped, his smile growing as he scanned me from my hair to my shoes. "You're beautiful, beautiful." He offered me his hand. "Are you ready?"

"For?"

"Your parents are here."

My chest grew heavier. "Mia said they were on their way." I looked up at my husband. "That's better than their house, right?"

"We'll face them together."

TWENTY-ONE

Camila

With Dante's hand reassuringly in the small of my back, we descended the staircase. "You're trembling," he whispered.

I was. My hands were also ice cold. The aroma of food met us as we stepped onto the first floor, twisting my already-nervous stomach. The din of voices faded as if we'd walked onto a stage already filled with characters.

Sergio, Papá's bodyguard, stood near the front door. I longed to ask him about Miguel. Instead, I stayed at my husband's side. My mother was with Mia near the food, Viviana was tending to something on the kitchen island. Jano, Em, and Papá were outside, probably discussing last night's attack.

Mama turned toward us. Her bloodshot eyes scanned over us as I leaned into Dante. *"Me partiste el corazón."* She clenched her heart.

"Tu rompiste el mio." I held back the threatening tears, praying I could keep them at bay. "I love Dante. I tried to tell you, but you wouldn't listen."

"Rei es un buen hombre."

"I don't love Rei."

Mama came closer. *"No quiero perderte como perdí a Catalina."*

She was purposely trying to keep Dante from our conversation. I wouldn't let her. "You're not going to lose me, Mama." I took a step away and wrapped her in a hug. Her arms encircled me as I basked in her familiar perfumed scent.

My nerves relaxed as we embraced. Maybe this was going to go better than I feared.

Papá appeared at Mama's side. Releasing her, I turned to him, hoping for a hug.

Before I could speak, his palm contacted my cheek. Shocked and stunned, I stared in his direction.

His gruff voice reverberated through the first floor. *"Avergüenzas a tu familia."*

Standing at least four inches taller than my father, Dante materialized at my side with a deadly expression as he seized my father's wrist. "Touch my wife like that again, and I'll kill you."

No.

This wasn't what I wanted.

Gasping, I jumped back and covered my lips with my fingertips. Dante held tight; his fingers blanched as he applied more pressure. Neither man spoke as they both stared at the other. To the side Sergio and Silas both had their guns at the ready.

"*Calma*," Jano said loudly, lifting his hands and coming closer with Em on his heels. "Dante, Andrés is a guest in our house."

Dante dramatically released his hold.

"*Bajen las armas*," Jano said, speaking to the two guards.

Begrudgingly, they re-holstered their weapons.

Papá's gaze flitted from Dante to me and back. Perspiration dotted his brow, and his face took on a red hue. His dark eyes weren't the ones I'd seen throughout my childhood. Warmth and love were replaced by a harsh coldness I'd never seen. "We are leaving." He turned to Mama. "Now." He reached for me. "Your marriage is over. You're coming with us, home, where you belong."

Dante and Jano both stepped between us.

"Andrés..." Jano tried.

Dante pulled me behind him. "You will never touch my wife again—ever." My husband was larger than life, as if he'd grown inches in height and width within the last few seconds. With his jaw clenched and his chest puffed, he was an over-two-hundred-pound wall of muscle separating me from my father.

Everyone in the room, most of the first floor, held our collective breaths as Dante and my father stared at one another. In this moment, they weren't family but stone-cold killers, each sizing up their prey.

"Camila."

It took me a minute to recognize Mia's soft voice. When I turned to her, she motioned with her chin for me to come to her and flee from the impending fury.

"No." I moved between Dante and Papá. "Stop this. I'm an adult."

"Then act like it," Papá said.

"I am. I made my decision. Dante and I are married, legally wed. The ceremony was performed by Father Gallo." I turned to Mama. "I'm married to the man I love." I tilted my head. "Isn't that what you want for me?"

"We'll discuss it at home," Papá said. Then he turned back to Dante, his voice sending chills down my spine. "You threaten me? I should kill you for what you've done. Camila was promised to another. *El Patrón* will deal with your capo."

Veins popped to life in Dante's neck as he stared back at my father.

"Valentina and Camila," Papá said, "we're leaving now."

"My wife stays with me."

Silas looked up from his phone. "The capo and Mrs. Luciano are here, coming through the gate."

Jano spoke. "We will take this to my office. Mia, please see to our female guests."

I turned on him. "You think that you can go into that office and decide my fate." My temper grew. "I have a news flash for you. This is the twenty-first century. I have the legal right to determine my own future."

Dante reached for my hand, his tone more reassuring. "You made your decision, Camila. It will be honored."

Silas opened the front door.

Catalina entered with a forced smile, a step ahead of her husband. Dario's gaze zeroed in on his brother and our intertwined hands as he assessed the scene. Armando, Catalina's bodyguard, was the final person to join our gathering.

"Mama," Catalina said gregariously, coming toward us.

Dario greeted Aléjandro. "Thank you for inviting us to your home. I sense some tension."

"You've always been perceptive, brother," Mia murmured from across the room.

After hugging Mama, Cat turned toward me. "Congratulations."

"You're the first person to say that."

Dario ignored Mia's comment as he turned to Dante. "You and I will talk. Then we will talk to the others."

No one argued.

No one else spoke.

The capo was here.

Catalina reached for my hand as Dante and Dario walked toward the front door. She lowered her voice. "You know how to cause excitement."

"I wasn't looking for excitement." I looked around. "Where is Ariadna Gia?"

"She's home with Contessa. Flying messes with her sleep schedule."

"Oh," Mama replied, "I wanted to see her."

"Then come back to Kansas City with us for a while. Give Papá time to calm down."

Mama turned to me, her voice cracking with emotion. "You married without me."

"*Lo lamento*." It was as I looked around that I realized the other men had gone back out to the pool deck.

Catalina too scanned the living room and out to the pool deck. "Mia, I'm so glad you weren't hurt last night. That must have been frightening."

"She was great," I said. "They were prepared."

"More than Rei," Mia said. "According to Aléjandro, his house needs tens of thousands, if not hundreds of thousands, in repair."

Catalina smiled. "It sounds like Rei will be too busy for a wedding."

I lifted my left hand. "I'm already married."

"Would anyone like to see the pictures from last night's ceremony?" Viviana asked. "I can show them on the television."

"I would," I said.

Cat, Mama, and I sat on the sofa while Mia and Viviana took chairs in front of the large screen. As Viviana broadcast the pictures to the bigger screen, Catalina whispered, "Dario is going to fight for you and Dante."

Her simple statement flooded my system with much-needed relief. "Thank you."

We turned to the television. The first picture was of Dante and Father Gallo beneath the archway of lights.

"My patio," Mia said. "I know it's only furniture, but it still hurts."

We all peered out the open windows to the empty space, devoid of furniture and all her stylish decorating.

"Oh, Camila," Mama cried at the picture of me emerging from the dark living room. "*Estabas hermosa*."

I remembered what Dante said about the moment when he saw me.

Everyone oohed and aahed.

"Emiliano," Mama said at a picture of him handing me the ring. She turned to me. "I'm sorry, Camila. I hope your father will listen."

I looked down at my ring. "I hope he does too, Mama. But whether he listens or not, I'm married to Dante."

"I took a little video of the vows," Viviana said before clicking *play*.

The voices came from the speakers.

Dante's voice filled the room. "Camila, receive this ring as a sign of my love and fidelity. In the name of the Father, and the Son, and the Holy Spirit."

I swallowed as he slid the ring over my finger.

My voice was next. "Dante, receive this ring as a sign of my love and fidelity. In the name of the Father, and the Son, and the Holy Spirit." Tears of joy filled my eyes as I watched.

Father Gallo spoke, "In the sight of God and these witnesses, I now pronounce you husband and wife. Dante, you may now kiss your bride."

Mama sat forward. "Did you see that?"

"Yes, I'm married."

"No." Her complexion was ashen. "Viviana, can you rewind it and go slower?"

"What are you talking about?"

Mama stood and walked toward the television. "Watch Father Gallo and Dante as you're placing the ring..."

We all stared.

"There, freeze it," Mama said.

"Oh my God." I got up and walked to my mother. "I didn't notice it before. I assumed it was a reflection."

Mama turned to us. "I know what that red light was. I saw it just before Luis was shot."

My stomach twisted. "Someone had our wedding literally in their sights."

"Why didn't they shoot?" Mia asked. She reached for my hand. "I'm glad they didn't, but why?"

"We need to show this to the men," Mama said.

CHAPTER

TWENTY-TWO

Dante

I followed Dario out the front door. The benches and flowerpots that had been decorating the courtyard were gone, cleaned away by Silas and Viviana, making the space look empty.

Dario turned, facing me, his stern expression giving nothing away. He was in capo mode. I knew this side of my brother. However, usually we were on the same side of whatever situation. "Tell me about the attack."

"You don't want to yell at me any more about my wedding?"

"I think we covered that on the phone. I would like to know what was happening between you and Andrés when we arrived."

"He slapped Camila, and I threatened to kill him if he ever touched her again."

Dario closed his eyes, and his nostrils flared. When he looked back at me, he had a slight shake of his head. "You're going to need to work that out."

"He slapped Camila. She deserves an apology. He also told Jorge he wants the alliance ended."

"He's upset. The alliance isn't ending."

"Maybe he's dirty like Gerardo was."

"Christ, Dante. Are you forgetting that he's my father-in-law too? He's Catalina and Camila's father. He's not dirty."

"You said *too*. You're acknowledging Camila and I are married?"

"You were smart to have a priest. It gives me something to work with."

"Camila deserved a real wedding even if it was rushed."

Dario crossed his arms, the sleeves on his suit coat pulling taut across his shoulders. "The attack."

"We heard the helicopter before we saw it."

"You said there were three men inside the copter?"

I nodded. "Pilot, copilot, and the door gunner armed with an MP5 submachine gun."

"MP5 doesn't exactly narrow anything down. They're used by militaries around the world, including Naval Spetsnaz." When I didn't respond, he added, "Russian commando frogmen. They're equivalent to our Navy Seals."

"Aléjandro said there was recently a shipment stopped at the border. Homeland Security tried to associate it with the Roríguez cartel, but it wasn't them. It was the Kozlov bratva."

"The same group responsible for the attack on the Ruiz home a few months ago." Dario's forehead furrowed. "Did the bratva plant the shipment to purposely incriminate the cartel?"

"I didn't ask. Eight hundred rounds a minute were raining down on this house."

"Bulletproof windows. Glad we're high in the sky or I'd want to invest in some."

"If you and Catalina move to the Ozarks, you might consider it."

"What makes you think I want to leave the city?" he asked.

"There's no yard for Ariadna to play in."

"There's a park." He shook his head. "I'd only consider it if we could move our mother someplace else." Dario exhaled. "I want to talk to them inside about the attack before Jorge arrives. First, we need to settle the wedding thing."

"The wedding thing is settled." I lifted my left hand. "I'm married."

"Let's go inside and convince Andrés so we can utilize the resources of both organizations to once and for all eliminate this Russian threat."

"I'll do whatever is possible to keep Camila safe." I thought about it. Despite Andrés's reaction, they were my wife's family. I reconsidered. "All of them."

"And all of us. Mia is still famiglia."

"Okay, my capo, I'll do whatever I can."

"Talk to Andrés. No shouting. No knives, guns, or threats of violence. Talk."

"I'd rather infiltrate the Kozlov bratva."

The front door opened, and Catalina smiled in our direction before her expression turned serious. "Hey, there's something you two should see."

"Hey," I said, going to her and wrapping my arms around her. I lowered my voice as we walked into the house. "I'm pretty sure I have you to thank for my brother not killing me."

"I don't think killing was on the table, but maiming was."

"Thank you."

Everyone was standing in Aléjandro and Mia's living room around the large television.

Dario's eyebrows knitted together. "We've gone from bloodshed to watching the wedding video?"

"There's a video of our wedding?" I asked, going to Camila.

"Yeah," she replied with a smile. "Viviana took it. But Mama noticed something."

Em, Andrés, and Aléjandro were standing the closest to the screen. Aléjandro turned. "Come fucking see this. I don't know how we missed it last night."

Dario and I walked closer.

"A red dot sight," he said. My brother reached for my arm. "It's fucking on you."

"And the priest," Aléjandro said. "Briefly, and then you can hear the helicopter, and we all go inside."

Dario turned to Valentina. "You spotted this?"

She nodded. "After Luis...I'll never forget that light."

"They had a red dot sight when your home was attacked?" Dario asked.

Camila's mother nodded. "I see it in my nightmares."

Dario continued questioning, "You definitively connected those attacks to the Kozlov bratva, right?"

"And Herrera," Aléjandro added. "Gerardo was working for Herrera."

Elizondro Herrera wanted to take over the Roríguez cartel, to incorporate it into his organization. Dario's gaze lingered for a few seconds on Catalina's. Right after they were married, Elizondro's wife invited Catalina to her hotel suite. Thankfully, it was exactly what it appeared to be—two old friends. Dario had feared it was a trap to steal his new wife to Mexico.

"Let me see that frame again," I said, taking in the video. "Viviana, where were you when you took the video?"

"I was sitting behind Jano and Mia."

"Come with me," I said to the masses, leading them out onto the pool deck. "The helicopter came from the ocean."

Everyone nodded.

"That laser sight—"

Aléjandro turned, looking at his own roof. "It came from this direction."

"Our guards were on patrol," Silas said. "No one was on the roof."

I looked around. "It's hard to judge without any of the furniture, but Viviana, can you estimate where you were seated?"

She walked to a spot.

"Camila," I said, "we were about..."

213

She came forward and walked toward the edge of the patio, the ocean breeze blowing her long skirt and the small hairs around her face. "About here. It was where the arch was." She turned and pointed. "I came out that door."

Silas stood peering toward the sky in different directions. "Red dot sights are typically used for closer ranges, 100 yards or less."

"Depending on the rifle," Em added, "they can be adequate up to 300 yards."

We were all looking up at the roofline. "If the shooter wasn't on your roof, with the way the second story obstructs a straight view..." I looked from Viviana to Camila. "There. Someone was on your neighbor's roof or in that window." I pointed. "That's the only possible vantage point."

"Do you know your neighbor?" Andrés asked.

"I've met the wife," Mia said. "Only once."

Walking to Camila, I wrapped my arm around her. I did it without thinking because she looked chilled. After I did, I noticed Andrés turning away. "Why would Kozlov send a sharpshooter and a helicopter?"

"Why didn't they shoot?" Andrés asked.

"Because Dante and the priest weren't the intended targets," Dario said.

"If those shots would have happened," Camila said, "right before the helicopter, the sharpshooter would have gone unnoticed. The submachine gun would have obliterated the body or bodies."

I hadn't noticed Silas stepping inside, but we all noticed his return and the man at his side.

Jorge Roríguez lifted his hands. "You are all getting along better than I anticipated." He went to Mia and gave her a hug. "*Hija.* How are you feeling, Mia?"

She smiled back at him. "Well. Just tired."

"And my grandson?"

"We don't know. You may have a granddaughter in there."

"Roríguez men father boys. But I'd take a girl." He turned to the crowd. "What's happening out here, where yesterday my son's home was attacked?"

Dario and Aléjandro explained what we'd found, starting with the video. As they spoke, Silas sent guards next door to look for clues to determine if the sharp-shooter was where we suspected.

Camila reached for my hand and whispered. "Who would have thought I'd be happy about last night's attack?"

"They do seem to be more concerned about that than our marriage." As I spoke, Jorge turned toward us. I lowered my voice. "We spoke too soon."

I pulled my shoulders back, remembering Dario's warning for me to make things right. "*Señor* Roríguez."

He offered me his hand. "Luciano. I didn't plan on another of our women going to the famiglia."

We shook. "I'm sure Reinaldo will find a wife."

Jorge nodded and looked at Camila. "He kidnapped you?"

"No, sir."

"He forced you?"

She shook her head. "No, sir."

215

"What did he do to convince you to disappoint so many?"

I squeezed her hand, fighting my urge to step in and answer for her, but I knew *el Patrón* wanted Camila's response.

"*El Patrón*," she said respectfully, "Dante made me feel special." She grinned up at me. "He loves me, and I love him. I didn't mean to disappoint anyone. I wanted to marry the man I love."

Jorge turned toward the multitude of eyes on us, everyone watching our interaction. "Andrés, you called for the end to the alliance."

Catalina gasped.

Her father's gaze went to her and back to Jorge. "I overreacted. Dario has stayed true. He's here today. I too am disappointed in Camila's decisions. I'm ashamed of her behavior." He looked at Valentina and sighed. "We know that she will be protected as Catalina is. As a father, that is what I want. My apologies to Rei."

"I spoke to him," Jorge said. "We will move forward." He turned to Dario. "We should talk, the two of us."

"You may use my office," Aléjandro volunteered.

After the two bosses walked away, Mia and Catalina rushed toward Camila as the three women hugged, pulling my wife from my grasp.

Remembering Dario's words, I inhaled and made my way to Andrés. "I hope someday you can be happy for Camila and forgive us." I offered him my hand.

For a moment, he stared at it. Finally, he took it. "Be a good husband. She has a wild streak in her. She needs more discipline than I gave her. Don't let her age fool you into thinking she'll be easy to control. She's not her sister."

A smile curled my lips and lifted my cheeks. "I wouldn't want her any other way."

Silas returned. "Jano, we found more than we anticipated."

TWENTY-THREE

Dante

We all turned to Silas. "Everyone, go inside. *Por favor.*"

"What's happening?" Catalina asked.

Mia and Camila shook their heads as I put my hand in the small of my wife's back, and we filed back into the house. Silas promptly closed the glass doors.

"Is everything all right?" Mia asked.

"If you and Jano could come with me."

Mia gave us one last glance as she followed Silas down the hallway leading to his and Viviana's suite. Beyond the large glass doors, cartel soldiers patrolled.

"Something is happening," I said, my grip of Camila's waist tightening. "I want to get you back to Kansas City."

Her gaze went to her parents, who too were having their own conversation. "I want to go," she replied. "But I want to know that everyone here is safe."

A few minutes later, Mia and Aléjandro returned. Mia's complexion was pale as she took a seat on the sofa. My brother-in-law's dark stare met mine. "Come with me."

One last squeeze of Camila's waist and I followed Aléjandro to his office. He nodded to Jorge's guard before he knocked once on the door. Without waiting for a response, Aléjandro led me inside.

Dario and Jorge were seated in comfortable chairs in the corner. They both stood as we entered.

"We have a situation," Aléjandro began.

I leaned against the wall with my arms crossed and the other two men retook their seats as Aléjandro spoke.

"When I purchased this house, Rei vetted the neighbors. The house next door where Silas and a few of our men just were is or *was* owned by a commercial realty firm. At the time of our moving in, it was rented by a couple, Micah and Jennifer Goodin. He's an investment banker, and she's an influencer. Mia was certain that she spoke to Jennifer at least once.

"According to Silas, upon first inspection, there is no sign of the Goodins. Their possessions are still in place. There is spoiled fruit on the counter as if no one has been present for a period of time. There are two cars in the garage. There was a surveillance system; it has been disabled. In an upstairs room, Silas found a complex computer setup. That room has a straight view of the front of our pool deck. It is most likely where the shooter took aim."

"Any weapons?" Dario asked.

"Silas has returned to the house to do a more thorough search, and I called Rei to do what he does and see what more he can learn about the Goodins."

Aléjandro pulled his phone from the pocket of his blue jeans. "It's Rei."

"That was fast," I replied.

"He's good at what he does." Aléjandro answered the call. "Rei, you're on speaker. Our *padre*, Dario, and Dante Luciano are with me."

I stiffened at the sound of my own name. The man on the other side of this call was supposed to marry my wife, and now we were fighting the same fight.

Reinaldo didn't acknowledge my presence. "I found some interesting information. Jennifer Goodin hasn't posted to her Instagram account or YouTube channel in over two weeks. Prior to that, she posted multiple times a day."

"What did she post about?" Jorge asked.

"Get this...she had a true-crime podcast."

"Fuck," Aléjandro growled. "Anything about us?"

"No, she was concentrating on a story out of Simi Valley. A woman, Kira Ivanov, was murdered after claiming her husband went missing. Jennifer believed the two incidents were connected, but the police weren't making any headway."

I looked at my brother-in-law. "Does that have a connection to the cartel?"

"*Sí*," Jorge answered. "Ivanov. Danill Ivanov was

Kozlov's soldier that gave up Kozlov's location after the attack on Andrés's home. Kira was his wife. He never returned to the bratva."

"Who killed his wife?" Dario asked.

"Not us," Aléjandro said. "When we were questioning Danill, he said the bratva would kill her if they knew he gave up information."

Dario stood. "Let me get this straight. Some random influencer living next door to you was doing podcasts about a bratva killing and didn't know she was messing with a powerful crime organization? And two weeks ago, she and her husband fell off the grid?"

"Yes," Rei answered through the phone. "And Micah Goodin has not reported to work in the same amount of time."

"No one has reported them missing?" I asked.

Rei responded. "The investment firm notified the police, and Jennifer's fans are commenting on her posts. The fan theory is that the two went away on a trip to investigate one of Jennifer's leads."

Jorge stood. "Get our people out of that house. We don't need any connection to whatever happened to the Goodins."

Aléjandro replied, "We need to know who was in that window with their sights on our pool deck. Whoever that was knows who lives here and is a danger to my wife and family."

Rei spoke. "I just accessed Micah Goodin's bank account. The day before his disappearance, he received a half-million-dollar wire transfer from an LLC out of Delaware."

"Always fucking Delaware," I murmured under my breath.

Dario looked up from his phone. "I sent Lorenzo, our trusted technology expert, the information Rei's found. Two searches are better than one. In the meantime, I propose that we take Valentina and Mia back to Kansas City with us."

The muscles in the side of Aléjandro's face tightened.

I asked, speaking to Dario, "When Herrera was in Missouri for your wedding, didn't he spend time in New York?"

"Yes."

"New York isn't far from Delaware."

My brother shook his head. "You can set the LLC up from anywhere. You don't physically need to be in Delaware."

"Of course Herrera has LLCs," Jorge said. "There's nothing linking him to any of this. Since Gerardo's execution, he's been quiet."

"We know Gerardo was working between Herrera and Kozlov," Aléjandro said. "Gerardo's out of the equation. Herrera and Kozlov are still present."

Rei spoke, "I found a deleted Instagram post, dating back to two weeks ago. It's a picture of Jennifer on a private plane. The caption reads 'Research.'"

"Any way to identify the plane?" I asked.

"I'll send Jano the pic. It's pimped up, but I'm not sure of anything else."

"The date of the post?"

As Reinaldo replied, I sent the information to Lorenzo with the message: *Scan manifests from private airports within a hundred-mile radius of San Diego for a flight with Jennifer Goodin on this date or the day before.* After I hit send, I looked up at my brother. "I have Lorenzo searching private airports in the area for manifests. If Jennifer Goodin is on there, he'll find it."

The five of us—including Rei—continued to brainstorm. The answers felt like they were fucking close. However, other than our assumptions, we were still in the dark.

"I had a visit from the police this morning," Rei said. "Jano, they took the story at face value."

Aléjandro scoffed. "It's easier for them to close a case than to keep it open."

"What story?" Dario asked.

"A similar one to what we told SDPD last night. We were paid by Sony Pictures for allowing them to use our homes in a movie scene. No one was in danger."

"And they fell for it?"

"Like I said," Aléjandro replied, "they have enough shit on their plate. Give them a feasible story and let them close a case and everyone is happy."

"Ingenious," I said.

Aléjandro grinned. "It was your sister's idea."

"Ingenious but not fucking true," Jorge said. "Both my sons were attacked. Link the attacks to someone, and we're going to shoot our own damn film of them going down."

CHAPTER
TWENTY-FOUR

Camila

Armando drove the large SUV toward the airport. Dante was in the front passenger seat, Dario, Catalina, and I were in the back seat. Mama and Mia were following in another car driven by Miguel with Em riding shotgun. I'd even had a chance to go back to my parents' home and fill multiple suitcases. Dante promised the rest of my things would be packed and sent to our new place.

My husband also filled me in on what happened in Jano's office. Talk of our marriage disappeared as the threats to the cartel were uncovered and discussed. He said Rei had been on the phone, and I was never mentioned.

Having the men in business mode was an appreciated reprieve.

The decision to take all the women to Kansas City, like most decisions, had been made without our input. Nevertheless, I was happy to be going. Mama and Mia would stay upstairs in Dario and Cat's apartment, leaving Dante and I alone to navigate whatever our future will mean.

Once we were on Dario's plane, we four women went to the back, sitting in a grouping of four seats while Dario and Dante continued to talk about the fires at hand. The Roríguez cartel wasn't the only one dealing with troubles. Between the Russians and Taiwanese, there was always an enemy at hand, an organization attempting to take over land, money, customers, and businesses.

Cat laid her hand on my knee. "How are you?"

"Glad to be headed to Kansas City. I was nervous about Papá."

Cat turned to Mia. "Thank you for helping Camila. She told me all you did."

Our sister-in-law sat taller. "I'm tired of being treated as if we can't make our own decisions. We have more to offer the famiglia and cartel than we can as trophy wives." She lifted her hands. "I know, my mother is one of the best. She can name every store on Rodeo Drive in Beverly Hills or Fifth Avenue in New York. I'm fortunate that Aléjandro listens to me." She looked at Cat. "You've done this too. Dario listens to you."

Cat nodded and looked at our mother. "He talks to me, something I never heard Papá do with you."

Mama inhaled, pushing back against the chair. "We say more in private. I suppose that is something we should have done more of in front of you when you were children. Andrés listens. I also know my place."

"It's not about place," Mia went on. "We're their *partners*, whether we chose that position or not. I want to make a difference."

"You are with the workers at the club," I said. "And you did with me."

"We can make small but significant contributions to achieve our own dreams." She laid her hand over her midsection. "When Camila explained her situation, I went to Aléjandro. I respect his position in the cartel and our family, but I didn't ask. It's a new thing for me. It wasn't that way before. I explained and reiterated my stance to let women be involved in the marriage discussion." She shook her head. "I don't believe Rei would be a bad husband. Someday he will be a great one. I'm not sure he's ready to marry now. I think it was Andrés working to prove to Jorge that he wasn't Gerardo."

"He's not," Mama replied. "He's not Gerardo. To me, Rei was the better choice because you knew him." She smiled in my direction. "I didn't know you knew Dante."

"Speaking of knowing him," Cat said, "when I asked how you were, I wasn't talking about going to Kansas City. I was talking about...well, if you were married last night, how did after the wedding go?"

Warmth crept from my neck to my cheeks. "I'd say my expectations were low. I mean, you told me it gets better." I looked at Mia. "You weren't all that optimistic either. I expected terrible." My smile grew. "It wasn't terrible."

Mia grinned. "Who knew my brothers would turn out to not be the asshole our father was?"

Cat reached for my hand. "I'm so happy to have you close. Oh, you can spend time with Ariadna Gia and me."

"I want that. I'm also going to keep up with my classes."

Mama's eyes widened. "You asked Dante?"

"Not really. It was more of a discussion. He said he'd agreed to that stipulation when Dario and *el Patrón* were in negotiations for me."

"Good for you," Mia said. "I'm going to spend the next week catching up with Giorgia and Mom. I'm excited to be back in Kansas City, but I don't want to be gone from Aléjandro for too long."

The sun had set by the time we landed, and our clocks went forward two hours. As others deboarded, Dante came back to me. Once we were alone, he grinned his handsome smile. "I'll carry you over the threshold of our apartment."

Inhaling his heavenly spice and leather scent, I laid my palms on his shoulders. "You don't need to carry me. I can't wait to be a couple, a real couple."

As our lips made contact, the stress of the last few days eased as if my body was releasing our past and making room for our future.

"I can't wait to have you alone, Mrs. Luciano. If you're still sore, we can find other ways to bring you to orgasm."

I tilted my forehead to his chest. "Is it bad that just hearing you talk about it makes me wet?"

He lowered his face to the crook of my neck, inhaled, and moaned. "I can tell. You smell of cinnamon and sex."

"You can't tell that from my neck."

"I can. Your sex pheromones are sweet and make me fucking hard."

Swallowing, I shook my head. "Are you teasing me?"

"Not yet." He took a step back and reached for my hand. "Come, let's get home and let the teasing begin."

There was a chill in the night air as we stepped out of the fuselage. "Where is everyone?" I asked, looking out at the tarmac and seeing only one car, a green Aston Martin.

"I told Dario I wanted to drive you home without company."

"What about my suitcases?" I was relatively certain they wouldn't fit in the car on the tarmac.

"They took them. Armando will deliver them to our apartment."

My smile grew as I lifted my face to the sky. "We really did it." I looked up at his handsome features. "We're married."

"We are." He gestured toward the car. "Your chariot awaits."

"Surely, this car hasn't been waiting here since you flew to California."

Dante opened the passenger door for me. "I had Giovanni bring it here and take back the car I drove yesterday."

The interior smelled of expensive leather. Most of the interior was soft and velvety to the touch. I watched with appreciation as Dante folded himself into the driver's

229

seat and gripped the steering wheel. "Will I be able to drive this car?"

His smile quirked. The dashboard illuminated with a green glow, matching the color of the exterior paint. "We have a lot of cars to take your pick. You might want something with a little less horsepower."

"You don't mind me driving?"

"I saw your license yesterday. I assume you passed a test."

"I did, but Catalina always has her bodyguard. I figured..."

He reached over, laying his hand over my knee. "Things to talk about, Camila. Dario is a bit paranoid. That doesn't mean you shouldn't have protection. I offered Miguel a job."

"What?" I asked as we glided across the tarmac. "Really?"

Dante nodded. "He said he'd need to think about it and talk to your father. After all, since Luis died, there's not been a steady bodyguard for your mother. Miguel was assuming that would be his position after you married."

"I was afraid Papá would blame Miguel for my absence."

The streets of Kansas City came to life around us. Tall streetlights illuminated the night sky. Buildings grew larger as we worked our way into the heart of the city.

"No matter who I hire to protect you, I expect you to stay with them. No middle-of-the-night escapes."

I raised my right hand. "No more middle-of-the-night escapes. Besides, won't I be busy in the middle of the night?"

Dante glanced in my direction, his dark gaze shimmering with the reflection of the dashboard. "Yes, you will."

As Kansas City passed by the windows, my thoughts went to our first night together. The day had been so eventful, I hadn't had a chance to reflect on what we'd done with and said to one another.

Dante pulled the car into the same garage I recognized from my visits to Cat's place. We made the same turn, entering the private garage, the area with the private elevator that went up to not only Dario and Cat's apartment, but the floor below, my new home.

Once the elevator doors closed, Dante spun me. My back collided with the sidewall as he pressed his hips against mine and lifted one arm over my head. Without a word, his lips sought mine, a strike of a match giving energy to the flames within me. A moan escaped my lips as we rose high into the Kansas City skyscape, and Dante took my breath away.

Our kiss didn't yield until the elevator stopped.

Blinking, I stared into his dark brown orbs. "You said the elevator has a camera."

"It does. If it didn't, you'd already be naked." My eyes darted around the seam between the walls and ceiling, searching for the recording device while wondering if he was serious about my nakedness.

The doors opened to the floor and apartment I'd only visited once. Taking my hand, Dante led me into our home. My suitcases were lined up in the entryway. The last time I was here, I was too nervous to mentally take in the surroundings. Much like the penthouse up above, Dante's space was filled with expensive minimalist furniture. Lights turned on as we entered the rooms, activated by motion sensors. In the living room there was a long white stone fireplace. With the touch of a button, flames came to life, flickering hues of orange and blue.

We turned the corner.

"This is the kitchen where you were first kissed," he said.

"And where I first kissed a man."

I ran my fingers over the cool quartz countertop and took in the glass backsplash and top-of-the-line stainless steel appliances. "Do you cook?"

"I make a mean bowl of cereal, and I've been known to burn toast. I'll have to demonstrate my culinary prowess to you in the morning."

"Lola, our housekeeper, taught me some recipes." I shrugged. "Cat cooks more than I can, but I'm willing to give it a try."

His smile curled. "Discussion for another day. There's a more important room I want to show you."

"More important than the kitchen. What in the world could that be?"

Dante led me through the living room to a hallway with multiple doors. He pushed the first one inward. "Bathroom." Second door. "My office." He turned on the light to a room, sans a desk and chair. "As you can see, I don't use it. I have an office at Emerald Club." He turned to me. "You should make it your office. A place to study and do your homework."

"Jano let Mia decorate their house."

"Aren't you studying interior design?"

My cheeks rose. "How did you know that?"

"Mrs. Luciano, it's my goal to learn all about you."

"My mysteries?"

He nodded. "You may change anything you want. I don't care if you gut the whole place and remodel. All I care about is that you're here and you are happy with your new home."

My grin grew. "This room has possibilities. I like everything else I've seen."

His eyebrows danced. "I'm glad to hear that. I like what I've seen too. There are two other bedrooms on the opposite side of the living room." He lowered his tenor. "Now let me show you the next room."

Dante turned the knobs on a set of double doors, opening them inward.

I gasped, my eyes growing wide at the sight inside.

The room flickered from the illumination brought on by a second fireplace. Words failed me as I stepped inside and spun, taking in the bouquets of flowers covering almost every flat surface. The king-sized bed was turned down and strewn with a colorful array of petals.

"How did you do this?"

TWENTY-FIVE

Camila

His deep voice hummed with anticipation. "I asked Contessa for a favor."

"You're sexy, dangerous, protective, and *romantic*? I think I hit the jackpot."

Dante stepped closer, his warmth radiating more heat than the fireplace. Snaking his arm around my waist, he pulled my hips to his. There was no hiding the bulge beneath his jeans. "I told you that I would spend my lifetime making you feel loved. I meant what I said. And as far as jackpots go, I'm the winner in this scenario. Now remember what I said would have happened in the elevator?"

My nipples grew taut.

"Me naked."

His stare simmered with a dangerous intensity as he nodded and reached for the hem of my shirt. "Lift your arms, Camila. I'm going to take my time undressing you, savoring each and every inch of your perfect body until I have you completely nude and laying open for only me."

He'd told me that in this bubble, he was in control.

I couldn't imagine it any other way.

Dante leaned closer, his warm breath washing over my sensitive skin behind my ear. "If you're sore, I can come up with other ways to spend our evening."

I inhaled, basking in his spice and leather aroma and looked up into his gaze. "Right now, I'm turned on."

"If you change your mind, just tell me." He lifted my chin. "I want to hear your thoughts and desires, Camila. I want to know what feels good so I can give you more."

I raised my arms in response.

Dante lifted my shirt, slowly pulling it over my arms and revealing my bra. The next piece of clothing to hit the floor was the orange skirt. Once he had me down to my bra and panties, Dante took his time, brushing his warm fingers over my flesh, kissing and nipping trails over my arms, neck, chest, breasts, and stomach.

My nipples drew hard as my bra landed on the floor.

The crackle of the fire combined with the deep baritone of his voice reverberated through me. His praises swirled around the bedroom as he voiced his appreciation for my body. Flint and steel created sparks that detonated beneath my skin. Lifting me from the floor, Dante carried me to the bed, laid me on the sheets, and tugged my panties down my legs.

Pushing my knees up and away, Dante brought his face to my core.

"I'll never tire of your sweet scent." He lapped from my back to my front, causing me to squeal and buck. With his arm over my hips, Dante held me captive, a prisoner to his vigilant ministrations.

No longer embarrassed, I gave into his attention, losing myself in his systematic disassembling of my preconceptions of intimacy. It wasn't like my mother was great at the talk. I asked more questions of Cat, but that was more academic than reality. Even the romance books I read failed to fully describe the closeness that came with this level of seduction.

I screamed out his name as my body quivered with the force of a California earthquake. There wasn't a play-book to tell me if I was ready for another round of inter-course, but that didn't stop the words from coming forth as Dante lapped my essence. "I want more."

Dante lifted his head, his dark stare searching for mine.

Lifting my head, I nodded.

"Fuck, Camila, I could get off listening to the erotic noises you make."

"I want you inside me."

Scooting up to the headboard, I leaned forward reaching for the hem of his t-shirt. "You're in charge, Dante. I'm fine with that. I just want to feel you, your body over mine."

I lifted his shirt, revealing the peaks and valleys of his toned abdomen. Spreading my fingers, I ran my palms over his broad shoulders, down his muscular arms. There were stories written in his scars and his strength, stories I could spend a lifetime learning.

Dante hastened from the bed, unfastening his dark jeans and kicking off his shoes and socks. As he reached for the waistband of his boxer briefs, I spoke. "I want to undress you as you did me."

I scooted to the edge of the bed. "I felt you last night and saw you this morning. I want to do more, explore your mysteries." I used his word.

"Fuck."

"You said to voice my wants and needs." I fell to my knees before him. "That's what I'm doing."

Dante~

I'D FUCKING DIED and gone to heaven. There was no other explanation for the fact that Camila was naked on her knees in front of me.

Speak her wants and desires.

That's what I'd told her to do. I hadn't expected this.

"Men aren't as complicated as women. It's not a mystery. Tasting you, listening to your noises, having you naked, and fuck, having you take me out makes me hard. When you touch me, I'll grow even harder."

Her lips curled into a smile. "Don't tell me all the spoilers."

"Oh, beautiful, those aren't spoilers. Those are facts."

She sat up on her knees, bringing her gorgeous face a little lower than my throbbing cock. Camila's tongue darted to her pink lips in a way that drew my balls tight as slowly, she reached for the waistband of my boxer briefs. My cock sprung free, released from the confines of the material.

Camila's emerald eyes widened as she stared.

"You can touch it."

She lifted her hands as if she were about to examine a rare ancient artifact.

A laugh bubbled from my chest. "Beautiful, you're not going to break it."

She looked up at me through her lashes. "I want to taste you."

Oh fuck.

The tip of my cock glistened with pre-come at the desire in her voice. If she didn't do something soon, I'd shoot my load all over her. "I'm all yours."

Her cheeks rose. "Mine."

"Fuck yeah, and you're mine."

Her hands approached my cock, their proximity caused my rod to go from hard to steel. I bit my lips as she closed her fingers around me and lifted me, her mouth coming closer to my cock. All at once, she lapped the tip. I swear on anything and everything that's holy, her tongue, only her tongue and I'm ready to explode. That one lick sent seismic aftershocks through my circulation strong enough to knock me off my feet.

Camila opened her lips and took me inside her warm, wet mouth.

Her tongue swirled around the tip before she took more and bobbed back.

"Fuck, your mouth is heaven."

She held tight to my thighs as she experimented with how far she could take me. Even her gagging sounds were erotic. The room filled with a pop as she pulled away.

I reached down and lifted her chin. "Have you ever sucked a cock before?" I knew the answer, but the primal beast within me wanted to hear her say the words.

"My first time."

Camila's trepidation eased as she went back to work. The room filled with a chorus of her moans, whimpers, and mews combined with my own curses. The curses came more rapidly. "Fuck, Camila. I'm going to come."

She again surprised me as she stayed on mission.

My restraint was gone as I reached for her head and pumped against her lips. A roar formed deep in my chest as I came, my seed spewing. My wife never stopped, swallowing everything I gave her.

Once we were satisfied, she looked up at me. "I think I did that right."

I offered her my hand to stand. "Another mystery solved. I came. You did that perfect."

Pink filled her cheeks. "It's okay if you can't...again. I mean, you are old."

"I'm old?"

Camila shrugged. "Older."

"Oh, little girl, I'll show you what I can do." I could definitely go again. My cock was hardening between us as we stood here. A little more roughly, I captured the back of her neck, forcing her to look up. "Tell me what you want."

"I'm...I want to try again. Even after coming earlier,

sucking you made me...I felt empty, and I want to feel full."

Stroking her hair, I stared into her gaze. "I don't deserve you."

Camila took my hand and tugged me toward the bed.

Following a step behind, I crawled after her, a lion sizing up his prey. Camila giggled when I seized her ankle and pulled her toward me. Kiss by kiss and nip by nip, I worked my way up. Her ankle, her calf, the sensitive skin behind her knee, up her thighs. I couldn't look her perfect pussy in the eye without one last taste.

Fuck, she was drenched.

I climbed higher, kissing and nipping until we were nose to nose. "I'll go slow."

Camila shook her head. "I want you inside me. I can take it."

My eyes closed as I slid my tip into her cunt. Opening my eyes, I took in her expression. Camila's eyes twinkled as she nodded. Our stares remained glued to one another's as I pressed farther into her tight, silken glove. Flexing my hips, I pulled out and thrust in. "You're good?"

She shook her head. "I'm better than good. I love that we're so close."

"I'm not sure closer is possible." I thrust in, and her back arched. God, she was stunning to watch. The angle of her dainty neck, the way her pert tits with their darkened areolas and hardened nipples pressed against me— they were all works of art. She was a masterpiece of untold value and beauty.

Our bodies followed the same dance, the music in

our heads as our heavy breathing and the slap of our skin created the overture. My thrusts came faster as the melody increased, the crescendo growing as the climax approached.

Camila's pussy quivered and tightened as her fingernails bit into my shoulders, and her lips formed the perfect "o." I was close. Too close. I pulled out, my come soaking the sheets in long white spurts mixing with the blood and come already present. "We need you to see Catalina's doctor because pulling myself away from you is one of the hardest things I've had to do."

Her satiated smile drew me to her. I fell at her side, wrapping her with my arm and bringing her head to my shoulder. I kissed her hair. She curled her body toward me, her fingers on my chest.

"I didn't realize how much I would like sex."

My smile returned. "I'm glad."

Camila lifted her head. "No, really. I do." She laid her head back on my shoulder.

"I was sensing that by the noises you made. Oh, and by the way your body convulses as you orgasm." I lifted her chin, bringing her swollen pink lips to mine. "Your dad warned me about your wild streak."

She cuddled closer. "I told you. We're married. You're stuck with me."

"You're not wild, Camila. You're made perfect for me." I took a breath. "I wasn't a big fan of the alliance in the beginning."

"You weren't?"

I shook my head. "Catalina convinced me more than any of Jorge's lieutenants or soldiers. But now, I'm so fucking grateful for the alliance. Without it, I'd never have met you."

"I love you."

"I love you, too." For the first time in days or weeks, my mind was clear. No matter what happened with the cartel or with the famiglia, the woman in my arms was mine.

Mine to protect.

Mine to love.

Mine to die for.

Camila's voice dripped with sleepiness. "Do you think the cartel will be all right?" She yawned. "I'm worried. That helicopter was brazen. Why would the bratva do that?"

As my wife drifted to sleep, her question repeated in my thoughts. The answer was so close. I just couldn't see it. Closing my eyes, I fought sleep as I replayed everything that had happened over the last few days.

There was something that Camila said.

Brazen.

Why would the bratva be brazen?

They wouldn't.

Someone who wanted the cartel to appear weak would.

Fuck, I needed to call Aléjandro.

TWENTY-SIX

Dante

Waiting on the tarmac, I watched as the cartel's plane landed at a small airport outside Kansas City. With my arms crossed, I leaned against my Aston Martin with a smirk on my face. A light jacket covered my holster and blocked the autumn chill in the air.

The seal on the plane released with a whoosh before the door opened, lowering the stairs. Aléjandro stepped out into the sunlight. Behind sunglasses, he scanned the tarmac, his gaze landing on me.

It had been a week since we'd flown home from San Diego ourselves, and a week since I called my brother-in-law with my theory.

Brazen.

Aléjandro shook his head as he came closer. "Nice car. Not as nice as my Porsche."

"Ten fucking times better than your Porsche."

He looked around. "I thought Mia might be here. You know I haven't seen her in a week."

"She wanted to come," I said, getting into the driver's seat as Aléjandro sat to my right. "I wanted a few minutes before other ears were around." I glanced in his direction. "What have you learned?"

"The manifest your man found had the Goodins on a plane owned by the same LLC that deposited the five hundred thousand in their bank account. Rei dug into the LLC. Whoever filed for the corporation did their due diligence to hide the true owner. It's buried under layers of corporations." He looked in my direction. "Who have you talked to about this?"

"You, Dario." I hesitated. "Reinaldo called me a few days ago."

Aléjandro nodded. "He told me."

"I should have been the one to clear the air about Camila." I should have been. I could blame the fact that I'd been bogged down in hunting for proof of Herrera's involvement against the Roríguez cartel. And then there's the fact I wanted to spend every waking moment with my new wife. Of course, business with the famiglia was always a factor, such as Emerald Club being raided a few nights ago.

Those would all be excuses. Reinaldo made the move, and I was humbled by his gesture.

"You two good?" Aléjandro asked.

"Yeah. He didn't know that I'd made a move on Camila."

"I mean, I knew. I didn't know that Andrés changed his mind or that Rei was in the running until that ball was already rolling. Glad you two talked. We all need to be together on this. If Herrera is behind it, we need to have proof. *Mi padre* won't make a move on another cartel without evidence."

"Our fucking father was the opposite. Blame, attack, kill, and then justify."

I headed the car toward the club to my office. "Lorenzo found something I want to show you before we head to the apartments."

Parking the car in the lot beside Emerald Club, Aléjandro and I walked toward the front door. "You've been here before, haven't you?"

My brother-in-law shook his head. "No, I've wanted to check it out, but the timing was never right."

"When Dario became capo, he moved his office to his apartment and upped security there. I always thought Rocco would take over the responsibility of Emerald Club, but..."

"Yeah," Aléjandro said with more than a side of sarcasm. "Things didn't work out so well for him. I'm not sorry."

"So, the club is mine, and I'm fucking spread too thin. I'm training a few of our trusted soldiers to run things here."

Enzo met us at the door. "Mr. Luciano." He nodded.

"Enzo, this is Mr. Roríguez, my brother-in-law." I

wasn't certain of Enzo's statistics or what qualified for the term giant, but he was damn close.

"Sir," Enzo greeted.

"Too bad you couldn't have found a bigger dude to watch the door," Aléjandro said, his gaze sweeping from the ceiling over the main portion of the building that went up three stories with catwalks and large spotlights in the rafters. Taking off his sunglasses, he studied the staircase that led to the second floor and windows that looked down from my office on the third floor.

"Second floor is VIP," I said, "Better liquor, private entertainment, and gambling. We were raided a few nights ago. ATF claimed they had proof we were facilitating the sale of illegal drugs, serving alcohol to minors, and profiting from prostitution."

"What did they find?"

"Not a damn thing. We have our contacts with KSPD who tipped us off. They caught wind of the warrant. We were squeaky clean."

Aléjandro laughed as we made our way to the elevator. "Someone deserves a payoff."

"Always."

We boarded the elevator, taking it straight to the third floor. My office was just off and to the right. "Come in."

"Nice," he said, looking around. He peered through the windows that looked down to the first floor.

"Through the back room, there's a view of the hallway to the private VIP rooms."

"ATF didn't question the private rooms?"

"We're a private club. If a member wants some alone

time with his or her friend or loved one, we offer the space. Maybe they just want some quiet time."

"Plausible answer."

I nodded. "Have a seat behind the desk. I want to show you what Lorenzo found." Aléjandro sat in my tall leather chair as I brought my computer to life. "His office is downstairs. We can talk to him later. He was having the same issues with the LLC as Reinaldo. Lorenzo decided to go another route and follow the money. He went back in time." I clicked the mouse and brought up the screenshots of the Goodins' bank statements. "You bought your house..."

"Right before Mia and I were married, May of this year."

"It was about that same time that Mrs. Goodin's influencer gig took off. She went big in record time."

"I don't understand," he said. "People like true crime."

"Influencers make their money in a variety of ways, commission through unique links, sponsored content, and ads. Jennifer had been at the whole influencer thing for over a year, but about the time you bought your house, she was targeted by some big money sponsors. At first, they looked legitimate, but as Lorenzo dug, he realized the money was coming from the same source."

"The LLC?"

"Exactly. The new sponsorship increased her visibility. It wasn't entirely responsible for her success, but it played a big role in getting her in the spotlight."

Aléjandro's forehead furrowed. "Get to the point."

"Lorenzo connected the money to Ivan Kozlov."

"Fuck. Not Herrera."

I shook my head. "Kozlov knows where you live."

"She was reporting on his bratva in her podcasts."

"Yeah, I bet he didn't see that coming."

The figurative wheels were turning in Aléjandro's head. "He lured them away and set up the computer system in the house next door." My brother-in-law stood. "Fucking next door to me."

"That's shut down, but Silas needs to fortify your security."

"Why go to all that trouble, be ready with a sharp-shooter, and send in the big guns at the same time?"

"He wouldn't. It's not the way the bratva works. They work more covertly. In my opinion, you were attacked on two different fronts that night. Kozlov's man was next door when the attack came on you and Reinaldo."

"Brazen," he said.

"We still don't have proof, but my money is on Herrera. He would benefit from the Roríguez cartel looking weak."

"We're not weak."

"Fuck no. Instead of surrendering or faltering, you went on, business as usual. You even married another of your princesses off to the famiglia. Nothing in that says weak. And the marriage shows the alliance is as strong as ever."

My phone vibrated. I looked at the screen. "I need to take this call." I walked into the back office and shut the door. Standing at the windows, I spoke. "Are you calling to tell me we're in for another raid?"

The informant spoke. "No. I thought you might want to know who reported Emerald Club."

"You have a name?"

"Valuable information, if you ask me."

I gripped the phone tighter. "You've already proven your worth. You know I'm good for it."

"Word on the street is that you're doing business with a cartel."

"What does that have to do with who reported Emerald Club?"

"If you ask me, you've been double-crossed."

"You have a name?" I asked.

"Juan Garcia."

"Fuck, you might as well say John Smith."

"Well, Juan is here on a legal visa, but Homeland Security is questioning his connection to a known cartel."

Fuck.

My thoughts went to my wife.

"Drug lord?" I asked, holding my breath.

"Elizondro Herrera. You owe me."

I let out a long breath. "I do. Can you get me physical proof? I'll pay extra."

CHAPTER

TWENTY-SEVEN

Camila

I lifted the mug of hot coffee to my lips as Contessa pulled the egg casserole from the oven, filling the kitchen with a delicious aroma. Ariadna Gia suckled at Cat's breast covered by a light blanket as Mama and Mia gathered around the kitchen table.

"I'm going to miss having you all around," Cat said, taking a drink of her herbal tea.

Mia looked at her watch. "I'll feel better once Aléjandro is here."

Mama's eyes shone as she watched her grand-daughter eat. "I'll be back." She turned to me. "Both of my girls living together." She tilted her head. "It makes me both happy and sad."

"I'm happy, Mama. I really am." My thoughts centered on the man who was now my husband. Even

253

though things had been busy since we returned to Kansas City, he'd spent any available time with me. Other than a few late nights at Emerald Club, he managed to make it home before I fell asleep. Having Mama and Mia in town, Cat and I have stayed content spending our time with them.

My only time away from the apartments was my doctor's appointment. Apparently, the name Luciano went a long way in Kansas City. Catalina's doctor's answering announcement said that she had a three-month wait to take new patients. A call from my sister, and I was seen that afternoon. Now as soon as I had a period, I was set with my first three months' prescriptions.

"When is Jano arriving?" Cat asked. "And do you know when you'll be headed back to San Diego?"

Contessa brought the casserole to the table. "Is there anything else I can get anyone?"

"You can have a seat," Cat said, "and sit with us. This smells fantastic."

"Oh, I have things to do, and I don't want to interrupt family."

"You're family."

Contessa smiled. "Let me know when Ariadna is ready for a diaper change and nap."

Cat looked down, tugged on the blanket and exposed her daughter's small head covered in soft dark hair. "She'll be tired after this." My sister looked up. "Mama, can you dish me a piece of that casserole?"

As Mama dished out pieces, Mia shook her head. "I'm going to stick with fruit."

Cat smiled. "I remember those mornings. What time is Jano arriving?" she asked again.

"He texted around eight Kansas City time to say he was getting an early start."

"What do you all say to going out for lunch? We could go to the Nelson-Atkins Museum of Art."

"Oh," Mia exclaimed. "I'd like that."

Mama furrowed her forehead. "Will Dario approve?"

"We'll take Armando and Giovanni. Ariadna will stay here with Contessa. As long as we have the bodyguards, Dario doesn't mind."

I sat forward, my smile growing. "Oh, I love that idea, too. We've hardly been outside, and I've heard so much about autumn in Missouri."

"You should see Arianna's place this time of year."

My elation morphed. "Yeah, my mother-in-law." With her home in the Ozarks. "Dante said she's upset that she wasn't invited to our wedding. He promised her when things quieted down, he'd take me to her."

Cat pressed her lips together. "Our mother-in-law can be—"

"A bitch," Mia volunteered. "But she'll get over it. Mom likes to make a statement." Mia smiled in my direction. "I talked to her when I spent the night and explained why the wedding was so rushed. Once she's done with her temper tantrum, she'll be all gushy."

Cat laughed. "I couldn't have said it better myself. In the long run, she'll have a better response than Papá."

Mama rolled her eyes.

"Okay," I said, bending my knee and sitting on my leg. "Lunch."

Everyone nodded.

Two hours later, I stepped into my closet, wrapped in a towel. While I'd thrown together a few suitcases of clothes, each time I started to dress, I thought of something else I didn't have. Despite Mia's declaration that we could be more than trophy wives, the idea of shopping was appealing. I'd meant to ask Dante if he'd gotten an answer from Miguel. It would be familiar to have him as my bodyguard, but at the same time, I was afraid he would still see me as the little girl he'd protected all my life.

Catalina had adapted to new bodyguards from the famiglia. I could too.

As I was deciding on what to wear, I turned, looking out the window. Missouri weather was new to me. Southern California was much more predictable. I checked my phone for the temperature and forecast.

Sitting on the edge of the bed, I saw a text message from an unknown number. The message was written in Spanish.

"HOLA CAMILA, escuché sobre tus emocionantes noticias. Espero que el Patrón no te haya obligado a casarte con un Italiano. Cat me dio tu numero. Llámame si Podemos ayudarte. Te deseo lo mejor."

PURSING MY LIPS, I shook my head as my mind filled with questions.

Who was this from?

Who did Cat give my number to?

Why did they assume I was forced to marry Dante?

Closing the text message, I chose not to respond. As Dante would say, it was a conversation for another day. Quickly, I checked my weather app. The forecast was for sunny and mid-seventies.

By 11:15, I was dressed and back up to Cat's apartment. Everyone was brimming with excitement at the prospect of going out into the world. The elevator filled with chatter as Armando took us down to the garage where Giovanni waited with a large three-row SUV.

The doors were extra thick, letting me know they were bulletproof.

"Oh," Mia said. "I can't sit in the very back."

"I can," I volunteered.

With the two guards in the front, Cat, Mia, and Mama sat in the middle and I climbed into the very back. Cat shared what she liked about the Nelson-Atkins Museum of Art. It was where we'd gone on my first visit to Kansas City. I remembered to ask my sister about the text message, but the thought was forgotten as everyone talked about the exhibits they wanted to see.

While Cat went on about their Monet exhibit, I remembered a jewelry exhibit from before. "Is the jewelry exhibit still there?"

"Oh, it is." My sister absolutely beamed when she could discuss art. It had always been her passion. "And for a few more months, there's an exhibit of male nudes from the 1800's."

"Have they changed since then?"

"I'm not that old," Mama said.

I was happy to be by myself in the back seat, as my mind went to my recent lessons on male anatomy. I doubted anything at the museum could rival the gorgeous male specimen now at my fingertips. While I was a bit embarrassed about my naiveté at first, Dante had eased my inhibitions. That didn't mean he wasn't amused by some of my comments. I'd seen the gleam in his eyes.

Last night, after he'd reminded me that I enjoyed our intimacy and he pulled me to his shoulder, I ran my fingers over his chest, memorizing every peak and valley and twirling my fingers in his chest hair. I was truly fascinated with the access he granted me to explore. I peppered kisses as I followed a lower trail of hair down to the penis that had been inside me.

"Camila."

"What?" I shook my head. "Sorry, I was daydreaming."

"I was telling Mama about the Rozzelle Court Restaurant. Do you remember it?"

"Of course, it's like a 15th-century Italian courtyard."

We all decided we'd eat lunch and then explore the exhibits. Armando and Giovanni stayed close and vigilant as we gathered our food and sat around a table for four.

"You know," Mama said. "We could host a reception for you and Dante. I'd prefer in California, but this place is beautiful."

I stabbed a piece of fruit. "We don't need a reception. We're married."

"I know, but you missed out on so much."

I looked around the table. "I know you all had big weddings."

Mia held up two fingers. "I had two."

"I don't need one." I covered my mother's hand. "I appreciate that you want to do that for us. You better talk to Papá." She shook her head. "But really, Dante and I are good. Mia and Jano know how to host a wedding with a bang."

"Oh." Groans came from around the table.

As we discussed which exhibit to see first, I peered around and whispered to Cat. "Where's the bathroom?"

She lifted her napkin. "I can go with you."

"It's okay. Just point me in the right direction."

"It's over there. Take Giovanni with you."

"Dario's paranoia is wearing off on you." I stood. "I'll be right back. Don't go see the male nudes without me." I shook my head at Armando and Giovanni and mouthed, "I'm good." After all, it was just the bathroom.

It was as I exited the stall that I felt the sting in my neck.

Before I could react, the world went black.

CHAPTER

TWENTY-EIGHT

Dante

"What the hell do you mean she disappeared?"

Giovanni's voice came through the speaker of my phone as Aléjandro and I raced from Emerald Club. "Sir, the women were eating lunch, and she went to the bathroom."

"By herself?"

"We could see the door. She said she was fine. Other people went in and came out, but Mrs. Luciano didn't come out."

My hands shook. "Her phone. Track her phone."

"We went in. We found her phone. It was in her purse under the sinks."

My brother-in-law stood in my way as I was about to

get into the driver's seat. "Give me the keys. You're in no condition to drive."

My heart was racing at over two hundred beats per minute. My hands were shaking, and I was seeing red, but I could fucking drive. "No. You don't know where the fuck you're going."

His nostrils flared. "Dante, get the fuck in the side seat. I can follow directions."

"We're headed to the museum."

Giovanni spoke, "I've called in backups. We have men canvassing the museum and the parking lot."

"She didn't just leave." My stomach twisted. "There's no way she would leave."

I took the passenger seat in my own fucking car.

"Tell me where to go."

"I'll program the GPS." I spoke to Giovanni. "We're on our way. Make sure the other women are safe and find my wife." I disconnected the call.

Immediately, my phone rang.

"Where the fuck are you?" Dario's voice roared through the car speakers.

"On my way to the museum."

"You shouldn't be driving."

"I'm here," Aléjandro said. "We were leaving Emerald Club when we got the call."

"Fuck. Good. I'm glad you're with him. Don't let my brother do anything stupid."

Aléjandro looked in my direction and grinned. "I stopped him from driving, but if we catch the mother-fucker, I'll help him murder whoever dared to touch Camila."

"Don't jump to conclusions. We don't know she was taken."

My volume was too high. "You think my wife of a week left me?"

"That's not what I said," Dario tried to pacify. "Try to do it without drawing attention to yourselves. I'll meet you there."

We disconnected the call.

Later that day, I couldn't have told anyone if the radio was on or what was said as my brother-in-law followed the GPS. The entire drive to the museum was hell. Multiple times, I contemplated getting out and running. I tapped my fingers on the window, needing to move, wanting to hit something.

His voice cut through the mayhem in my thoughts. "They'll find her."

"She didn't leave of her own free will. Why the fuck wasn't she being better watched?" I ran my hand through my hair. "Who did this? Who would be ballsy enough to take my wife?"

"Brazen," Aléjandro and I said together.

"I'll call Rei," he said, reaching for his phone in his pocket.

"His number is in my phone," I volunteered. Aléjandro hit the talk button on the steering wheel. "Call Reinaldo Roríguez."

"Calling Reinaldo Roríguez."

"Luciano," he said, answering on the first ring.

Aléjandro spoke. "Rei, I'm here with Dante. Camila has gone missing."

"What the fuck? She leave him already?"

I pounded my fist against the door handle. In another second I'd explode.

"Not good timing," Aléjandro said. "We just got some information on Herrera. Can you get us a location? Is he in the States or in México?"

"I don't know. He stays under the radar, like *Padre*."

"Like *Padre*," Aléjandro said slower. "Does Herrera have a boat?"

"If he does, it's buried under multiple corporations. If he's been in the US, he's supposed to report to CBP, but we know *Padre* avoids that. I'd assume Herrera would too. Let me ask around. If anyone's heard rumors, I'll let you know."

We disconnected the call.

"The museum is right up there," I said, pointing through the windshield.

My phone rang through the speakers. "I'm ready to throw this out the fucking window." Dario's name appeared on the screen. I hit answer. "What?"

"We're all in the parking lot around back. Come to us."

I looked to Aléjandro, who nodded.

"We're almost there."

My heart seized at the sight of Catalina, Mia, and Valentina. Their hair blowing in the wind. Catalina was talking with Dario while Armando, Giovanni, and other soldiers stood by. Valentina appeared to be crying. Aléjandro pulled my car up to their grouping.

I opened my door before he even cut the engine. "Why are you back here?"

Armando stepped forward. "Lorenzo is tapping into

the museum's surveillance. They have an extensive system with all the priceless artwork in there."

"I don't give a fuck about the art."

As Aléjandro went to Mia, Dario came closer, dressed in his designer suit. His diamond cuff links glistened in the sunlight. "Camila didn't come out of the bathroom or wasn't seen coming out. That could mean she was disguised or carried out."

"How the fuck wouldn't you have seen her?"

"I read an article," Mia said, walking with her husband, the two joining our group. "It was about people stealing children."

Camila wasn't a child.

After covering her midsection, she went on, "I want to know the possible dangers before our baby is born. Anyway, the article said many children are abducted in plain sight. They use wigs, hats, change their clothes... and sometimes, they drug the child, so it looks like it's sleeping. They can walk right by a parent who won't even recognize their own child. They say to look at shoes. Usually, they don't have shoes with the disguise."

Shaking my head, I ran my hand through my hair. "Camila isn't a child. No one carried her out of the bathroom."

"She's petite," Armando said. "The only thing that Lorenzo has seen outside the bathroom was a cleaning cart, one of those big ones with supplies and trash containers."

Dario pointed to the loading dock. "If someone took her, drugged her, put her in a trash container, it would make sense that they would use the loading dock to take her away."

I was fucking ready to vomit.

"I will kill the motherfucker..."

Dario laid his hand on my shoulder. "That goes without saying. Lorenzo is checking the cameras by the loading dock. If they haven't moved her yet, she could still be there, somewhere in the museum. We have six men searching."

"And if she's gone?" I asked through clenched teeth. "Then we're fucking wasting precious time."

"If she's gone, we will get a license plate."

"This all goes back to Herrera," I said. "I know it in my gut. The attacks in California. Kozlov was behind the sharpshooter that's MIA. The bratva doesn't do brazen, but Herrera would. The bigger and showier, the better. He wants to make a statement to Jorge and to you." I went on to tell Dario about the informant, the person who reported Emerald Club.

"Your KSPD informant isn't very bright if he thinks we're working with the Herrera cartel."

"We don't exactly advertise," Aléjandro said. "And to your cracker cop, we all look the same."

Mia held tight to her husband's arm. "Camila can't be too far away."

But they'd want to get her away.

I had an idea. "We need to send soldiers to all the private airports," I said to Armando. "Get a call out. I don't want one plane leaving Kansas City or surrounding areas without an inspection. Make it work."

Catalina came from the SUV. "Here's her purse and phone."

Lifting the small purse to my nose, I closed my eyes and inhaled her cinnamon scent. Swallowing back the bile rising in my throat, I opened her purse and pulled out her phone. "I don't even know her passcode."

"Let me see it," Catalina said, reaching out her hand.

I handed her the phone.

Catalina entered four numbers, bringing the phone to life. She handed it back to me with a grin. "When Camila was young, she found a cat and named her Bell. Papá wouldn't allow us to have pets, so she kept Bell in the pool house for over a month before the cat was discovered."

"Bell?"

"2-3-5-5, on the keypad."

"What happened to Bell?" I asked.

"Papá had his men take her away. We told Camila she ran away."

"Was she ever told the truth?"

Catalina shrugged. "I haven't thought about that story in years. I just know it's Camila's go-to passcode."

"I'm going to tell her the fucking truth and take her to the pound. She can have fifty cats if she wants. I don't give a damn. Our father wasn't fond of animals either. You all can start with kids. We'll start with cats."

Tears came to Catalina's eyes. "You'll find my sister."

"I will." I opened her text messages. My nose scrunched and I passed the phone back to Catalina. "What does this say?"

She read aloud, translating the Spanish to English.

CHAPTER
TWENTY-NINE

Camila

My stomach cramped as my world grew into consciousness. Slowly, the world around me infiltrated the inky fog surrounding my brain. I was moving, not me physically, my body was moving. I was in a vehicle.

When I tried to move, something sharp bit into my wrists as the putrid odor of smoke and perspiration filled my senses. My ankles too were restrained.

The sound of my heart thumped in my ears as I worked to control my breathing.

Wherever I was, I wasn't alone.

A quick blink of my eyes gave me a snapshot of my surroundings. I was still wearing the same capri pants and blouse I'd worn to the museum.

The museum.

I'd been eating lunch with my family.

Gritting my teeth, I recalled the stinging sensation in my neck.

The terror built around me, consuming me with the reality that I'd been kidnapped. Someone had taken me away from Dante.

I heard a man's voice speaking Spanish.

Another blink.

The floor beneath me was covered with dirt and trash. I moved my head. The space was confined. Behind a seat. I was behind the seat in a truck, concealed in plain sight.

I held my breath at the ringing of a phone. The seat in front of me shifted.

A man's voice filled the musty air. "*Jefe. Sí.*" A laugh. "*Demasiado fácil.*" He continued with pauses, his entire conversation in Spanish. "She's still out. I just checked."

I could only hear his side of the conversation.

"We got the signal when she started moving. It took us straight to the Nelson-Atkins Museum of Art."

"No, we dropped her phone."

"I'm sorry, boss. They won't even think to check it."

"Yeah, that text message downloaded the tracker immediately. Led us straight to her."

"Wait."

"The tracker is still working. It's still at the museum."

"They'll never catch up to us. We're almost to the airport."

"Should be there in a few hours."

Tears leaked from my eyes.

Whoever had me was talking to someone who wanted me.

That text message this morning.

Airport.

Where were they taking me and to whom?

"Dante," I said in my thoughts. "I love you. Please find me."

THIRTY

Dante

"Camila, I heard about your exciting news. I hope el Patrón didn't force you to marry an Italian. Cat gave me your number. Call if we can help you. Wish you the best." Catalina looked up at us. "I haven't given Camila's number to anyone, no one recently."

I tried to make sense out of the message. "I hope *el Patrón* didn't force you to marry an Italian. What the actual fuck?"

Catalina shook her head. "I don't recognize the number, and they didn't identify themselves."

Aléjandro took the phone and reread the message. "Someone from our cartel? Someone against the alliance?"

273

"Camila's friends wouldn't say I gave them her number. They would also come up with a name."

"Shit, fuck." I fisted my hair.

"Herrera?" Aléjandro asked.

"Ana?" Catalina questioned. "I haven't communicated with her since right after my wedding." She took the phone from Aléjandro. "No. Ana is in Mexico. This isn't an international number."

"Someone in California," Dario hypothesized. He typed something into his phone. "Yes, the area code 310 is California—Los Angeles and Ventura Counties and Santa Catalina Island."

Aléjandro hit my shoulder. "Catalina Island is nearly fifty miles off the coast. It used to be considered part of México, but now it's California."

"In international waters?" Mia asked.

"Yeah."

My words were more of a growl. "I'll fucking fly back to California."

"I'm going with you," Aléjandro said.

"No." Dario lifted his hands. "Not yet. Camila has only been gone for less than an hour. Armando had soldiers headed to airports. I don't want the two of you going off headstrong, causing a war with Herrera in international waters."

"I'm not interested in starting a war, just cutting off his balls."

My brother's nostrils flared as he stared at me.

"Fine, I won't get into a plane. But I can't stand around here any longer." I looked at my brother. "The women should be taken back to our home. Mia's pregnant and Valentina is a wreck."

Dario nodded. "Give Camila's phone to me. I'll take it to Lorenzo at Emerald Club. He should probably sweep it anyway. There might be some clues on there."

"Can he find out where the text message originated from?" I asked.

"I'll ask him."

I looked at Aléjandro with Mia at his side. "Stay with Mia. I'm going to head out to Lee's Summit. It's the airport the cartel used for the wedding."

"Did Herrera use it too?" Dario asked.

"I don't know, but I can't not be doing something."

Aléjandro kissed Mia's hair and turned to me. "I'm going with you."

"Take Nico and Luca," Dario said, motioning the two soldiers in our direction.

"Four won't fit in my car," I said.

Dario reached out his hand. "Give me your keys. I'll have Giovanni drive your car back. You take one of the sedans."

"My car's faster."

"You'd probably end up pulled over for speeding from some rookie cop who hasn't learned the power of the Luciano name. Then we're all fucked."

Aléjandro gave Dario the keys to my Aston Martin as I took the driver's seat of the sedan. My brother-in-law was at my side, and Nico and Luca sat in the back seat, armed like us.

"Lee's Summit is small," Nico said. "Hard to sneak in and out of."

275

"An international airport is hard to sneak in and out of," I said. "In a small airport, fewer people ask questions."

I met Luca's gaze in the rearview mirror. "Find out if Armando sent soldiers to Lee's Summit and let them know we're on our way. GPS says it will be twenty-six minutes." I turned to Aléjandro. "My Aston Martin is much faster."

About fifteen minutes into our drive, Luca received a call. "It's Enrico. He's at Lee's Summit."

Enrico was young, but a promising soldier in our famiglia. I had my eye on him to help run Emerald Club with Antonio. "Put him on speaker," I said, pushing the accelerator.

"Rico," Luca said, "you're on speaker. Dante is here."

"Boss, this isn't the right airport."

I struck the steering wheel with the butt of my hand. "Maybe they're not there yet."

"Could be. Only one vehicle has come in since we arrived. It's a rusty old Ford pickup truck. Bench seat. I checked the bed, nothing but junk. They don't speak English."

The hairs on the back of my neck stood to attention. "Spanish?"

"Yeah, how did you know?"

Doesn't exactly sound like someone who would be flying on a private plane. "What are they doing there?"

"We can't exactly have a conversation. They parked near a hangar with a Cessna 182."

That's not a big plane.

"Fuck," I growled.

"Don't let them take off. We're getting off 470."

"Got it, boss."

"Spanish," Aléjandro said. "Oldest trick in the book to pretend you suddenly forgot *Inglés*."

The speedometer went higher as I passed on both the left and the right, weaving around cars on the exit ramp and onto the two-lane road. Fuck the police. If they try to pull me over, they can follow me all the way to the airport.

To my side, Aléjandro pulled his gun from his holster, inspecting his weapon. Both of the men in the back were doing the same.

For better or worse, no one tried to pull me over.

Considering the firepower in this car, it was for the better. Taking out some rookie cop for doing his job would piss off the members of the KCPD currently on our payroll.

As soon as I brought the car to a stop, the four of us jumped out. We ran through the empty small airport out to the tarmac. The two men with the hand tug attached to the Cessna looked up at us as we ran toward them.

Their guns became visible too late.

Enrico was shot at close range.

"Fuck," I yelled, my gun pointed.

Aléjandro shot first, taking down one of the men. I shot the second in the leg as Luca shot the gun from his hand. "Don't kill him. I want information." I looked down at Enrico. They'd aimed at his head. I scrunched my nose, knowing he wasn't alive. Fuck, I hated telling wives their husbands were dead.

Aléjandro ran up to the man injured in the leg,

speaking in Spanish too fast for me to understand even if I could. The man was yelling back at him.

"Look in the truck," I said to our soldiers.

"Just junk in the bed, like Rico said."

"The plane?" I questioned, jogging to the open door. The four-seater plane was empty. "Goddamn it," I cursed, hitting the plane with the butt of my gun. The tin can echoed. I stopped, standing perfectly still. "Did you hear something?"

Aléjandro stood, kicking the man with his boot. "He's not talking."

"He's guilty of something," I said. "No one starts shooting who isn't."

"I can make him talk." Aléjandro's eyes darkened. "Do you know a place where we can have more privacy?"

"Gag him," I said to Luca. "Stop his bleeding. Bind his arms and legs and put him in the trunk of the car." I looked at the two dead men. "And call a cleanup crew. The boss doesn't like us to leave bodies."

I turned toward the plane, certain I heard a noise. I looked at Aléjandro. "Did you hear that?"

It was then I noticed the small door on the side of the plane.

"Cessnas have two small luggage-storage compartments. Not big enough for a person," Aléjandro said.

"Camila isn't a child, but she's not big." I walked to the plane and opened the door. "Fucking Christ."

My wife looked so fucking fragile as I pulled her from the compartment. Aléjandro had his knife unsheathed and quickly sliced the ropes binding her wrists and her ankles as I removed her gag. With her cradled to my chest, I walked around the plane.

My chest heaved with sobs.

I didn't cry.

I don't cry.

I hadn't fucking cried since I was a boy.

Crying was a hard no with my father.

Camila's hand palmed my cheek. "Dante, I love you. I'm okay. You saved me. I knew you would."

Although snot dripped from my nose and salty water leaked from my eyes, I kept my voice strong. "I thought I lost you." I extended my arms to see her in her entirety. "Did they hurt you? What did they do to you?"

She lifted her hands. Her wrists were red and chafed from the ropes.

"We'll get you home and call a doctor."

Again, her hand came to my cheek as she stretched her neck, bringing her lips to mine. She tasted like a fucking ray of sunshine and smelled of cinnamon.

"I can walk."

"No, I'm carrying you." I wiped my nose against my shoulder. "You're never leaving the house again."

"I heard them talking."

I kissed her forehead. "We'll talk in the car."

When we came from around the plane, Aléjandro was on his phone with a smile on his face.

"Mia?" I asked.

He nodded. "She'll spread the word."

"Tell her we're bringing Camila home. And you're driving." I watched as Nico picked the man off the ground, his hands and feet now bound. "Stuff him in the back of the plane and wait for the cleanup crew. Take him to Emerald Club, the basement." I looked at Aléjandro, and he nodded. "No one touches him. We'll be over later to question him."

I carried Camila to the car in front of the airport. She lay with her head in my lap as we settled into the back seat and Aléjandro got in behind the steering wheel. "Home, driver."

He met my stare in the rearview mirror. "Fuck you."

My cheeks rose in a smile as I stared down at my wife. "Do you sprinkle cinnamon on yourself after you shower?" I asked my wife.

"It's perfume. It's call Queens and Monsters by Henry Rose."

I smoothed her hair away from her beautiful face, inspecting her for any signs of injury. Whatever I found on her, the man headed to Emerald Club would feel five hundred times more. "Queens and Monsters," I repeated. "That's us." I looked up at my brother-in-law. "All of us. You, Catalina, and Mia are the queens."

"You're not a monster," Camila said.

She didn't know what I had planned for the man back at the club. I might not be a monster with the woman I loved, but there was a monster inside me, and he was coming out tonight.

CHAPTER

THIRTY-ONE

Camila

I reached for Dante's hand, holding it between both of mine. "When I woke, I heard the men talking to someone. They called him boss."

"Did they use a name?"

I shook my head. "They spoke in Spanish, telling the boss that they had me." I began to sit up and Dante eased me back to a lying position. "Fine. I know how they found me." He lifted his eyebrows. "This morning, I received an odd text."

"In Spanish. I saw it. Catalina translated it for me."

"The men said that when I opened the text message, a tracker was downloaded on my phone. They followed us to the museum and even knew when I went in the bathroom."

Dante shook his head. "How did they get you out of the museum?"

"I don't know." I brought my hand to my neck. "I felt a sting. It might have been a needle, but I didn't see anything. When I woke, I was tied up behind the seat of a truck."

"Behind the seat?" Aléjandro asked.

"I pretended to be unconscious, but before they put me in the plane, they added the gag."

I noticed Dante's expression as he looked up, as if he was communicating with Jano in some wordless conversation.

"Did they say where they were taking you in the plane?"

"I listened for a location, but I never heard one."

Dante lifted his face. "They had to file a flight plan." He took his phone from his pocket and spoke to the phone. "Check the airport. There had to be a flight plan filed for the Cessna." He hung up.

"Do people always do what you tell them to do?" I asked with a grin.

"Most people."

"Good to know."

I sensed the difference in lighting as Aléjandro pulled the car into the parking garage. Dante gave him instructions on how to access the private garage. Once Jano parked the car, I sat up. "I can walk, Dante."

"I'm going to be right beside you."

We rode the elevator all the way to the penthouse and were greeted by everyone. Even Contessa and

Armando were present. I received hugs all around as we made our way into Cat's living room.

"Mrs. Luciano," Contessa said, "what can I get you?"

"My name is Camila. Water would be wonderful."

She grinned. "Right away, Camila."

I drained the first bottle and had drunk most of the second by the time the doctor arrived. This was a different one than I'd seen for my birth control. Dante assured me that Dr. Barone was the famiglia's physician and wouldn't ask as many questions as other doctors might.

Dante and I went with the doctor to Dario and Catalina's bedroom suite. Instead of completely undressing, I removed my capris and shirt and covered myself with my sister's robe I found in the bathroom.

Dr. Barone was nothing but respectful as he inspected my skin. There were more bruises than I realized littering my arms and legs. The only open wounds were on my wrists from the abrasive rope. Questions were asked about a possible sexual assault. I literally felt Dante's intense gaze on me as I answered.

No. I'd recently had my first and many consecutive sexual encounters. I was certain beyond a doubt that I hadn't been raped. Even saying the word sent shivers over my flesh.

Dr. Barone drew blood to test for whatever drug was used to render me unconscious. He prescribed antibiotics and muscle relaxers, warning me that once the adrenaline in my system wore away, my body would become sore. He also recommended an antibiotic cream for my wrists and ankles.

After thanking the doctor, we joined the others in the living room. Dante asked if I wanted to go down to our place, but there was comfort in having my family all about. Dante remained omnipresent, until he received a text message.

"What does it say?"

He looked across the room at Aléjandro.

"You two are starting to freak me out. You have some kind of bromance going on?"

Dante shook his head and chuckled. "No, but we do have a common enemy, and later, we plan to bond over some carving."

"Carving?" I asked.

"Wood?" Mia asked.

"Something like that," my husband said. He looked at Jano. "Come with me to Dario's office. We just received confirmation on the flight plan."

"México?" Jano asked.

"Catalina Island."

DANTE~

DARIO'S SUIT coat was missing, and his shirt sleeves were rolled up. None of that diminished his aura of power and control, punctuated by his visible holster. He looked up as we entered. "How is Camila? What did Dr. Barone say?"

"She's going to be sore. There's more bruising than we realized when she took off her shirt and pants." My brother's eyes widened. "She wasn't sexually assaulted."

"Good."

"Luca," I said, "has the kidnapper at Emerald Club. We received confirmation on the flight plan. The plane was taking Camila to Catalina Island."

"And you believe there's a yacht out there flying the Mexican flag."

Aléjandro stepped forward. "I want to hear what we can get out of the fucker at the club, but if we're right, *Padre* needs to be involved in this conversation."

Dario nodded. "That said, Herrera is causing problems here too. This isn't just the cartel's fight."

"It's our fight," Aléjandro said. "All of *ours*."

I spoke. "I'm going to talk to Camila. I don't know if she wants to be downstairs all alone."

"She can stay up here as long as she wants," Dario offered.

"I planned," Aléjandro began, "to take Mia and Valentina back today." He looked at me. "But there's no way to know how long we'll be at the club."

"You and Mia can stay at our place," I offered. "We're safer here than in a hotel."

"Mia has been staying here," Dario said. "No sense in making her leave. Aléjandro, you're welcome in my home."

There were seismic changes happening in this alliance, as if the ground was shifting under our feet. "Either place. Choice is yours," I said.

"Call me with any news," Dario said as we turned to leave.

"Are you ready?" I asked.

Aléjandro's smile grew. "Let's tell our wives we'll be gone, then I'm ready."

The room where the man was being held wasn't on the tour we gave ATF. It was only accessible through the wine cellar, behind a wall of top-shelf bottles. As soon as the door opened, the stench of piss filled my nostrils.

"Fuck," Aléjandro murmured. "Next, he'll shit himself."

The man's head was down, his chin near his chest. His pants, that had been cut away from his leg wound, were wet as was the concrete near the chair. The drain in the floor came in handy when this room was bleached and sprayed down.

I walked closer, taking in the zip ties binding him to a metal chair with a makeshift bandage on his leg wound. I'd instructed the soldiers not to let him bleed out. This man had a full night ahead of him before death would offer a reprieve.

Aléjandro inspected the tools laid out on a table to the side of the small room.

"Good enough?" I asked.

He nodded. "I can make do."

The man stirred at the sound of our voices. His eyes widened as he cursed in Spanish. Hell, I don't know what he was saying; he might have been praying. If he was, he was angry at God. Aléjandro spoke to him, occasionally holding up tools: pliers, pruning shears and Fiskars, perfect for cutting fingers and toes, surgical scalpels, and dental extraction forceps.

As Aléjandro showed the man each implement, the color drained from our guest's face.

Finally, my brother-in-law said, "We're going to cut the bullshit and speak in *Inglés*. You see, I don't want my brother here to miss out on any of the information. And if you tell me you don't speak *Inglés*, we'll start with cutting out your tongue."

"*Hablo Inglés.*"

"Now we're getting somewhere," I said, removing my shirt. I looked over to Aléjandro. "I don't want to get blood on it."

He followed suit.

CHAPTER

THIRTY-TWO

Camila

M y eyes fluttered open as the bed dipped. Through the darkness, the fresh scent of bodywash filled my senses as Dante's warmth settled to my side. I reached out, laying my fingers on his warm skin. "You showered?"

My body shifted as he wrapped his strong arm around me and pulled me to his side.

"I did, beautiful."

His words vibrated in his chest. "What we did tonight was messy, not something you need to see." Peppering my hair with kisses, Dante inhaled, filling his broad chest with air. "You always smell so fucking good."

Tilting my chin, I looked up at his strikingly handsome profile. "I soaked in the tub before going to bed."

"I expected to find you upstairs."

"Giovanni is in our guest room."

Dante scoffed. "He was in our kitchen watching the elevator. I told him to go upstairs to his own fucking bed."

My smile grew. "He was out in the kitchen?"

"He's a good soldier and takes protecting Luciano women seriously."

"Have you heard from Miguel?" I asked.

Dante inhaled. "Your father wants him to stay in California. With all the shit going on with the cartels, Andrés wants his men close. I don't blame him."

I sat up.

There was a lot to unpack in Dante's statement.

"I'm okay with a new bodyguard."

Dante's large hand rubbed up and down my back. "You're not going to fight me on the bodyguard thing?"

"After today, hell no."

My husband's laughter filled our suite. "My wife is cussing. She's either having an orgasm or being definitive in her statement."

I felt my cheeks move upward. "Not orgasming. And I don't swear during sex."

In one fell swoop, my head was back to the pillow and a man made of solid muscle had me pinned to the mattress. "You do, beautiful, and I love to hear every word, noise, and sweet, sensual sound that comes from your lips. I wouldn't want you any other way."

Lifting my hand, I pressed it to his chest. "Tell me about the cartels. You're using the plural."

Dante inhaled and exhaled, his toothpaste-scented breath coating my face. "Tonight, we received confirmation on a theory Aléjandro and I have been working on since the attacks the night of our wedding."

I shook my head as dread bubbled into my bloodstream. "I've overhead Papá and Uncle Nick talking since before the alliance. They're not always talking about the bratvas. Their distrust goes further. They don't trust Elizondro Herrera. I remember how upset they were that he and Ana came to Cat's wedding. They blamed the famiglia."

Dante knitted his eyebrows. "Why in the hell would the Mafia invite a second drug lord to a wedding? One was more than enough." He shook his head. "Their suspicions were partially accurate. Herrera is a threat. He was behind your abduction. We got that directly from one of the abductor's mouths. Herrera was also responsible for the attacks on the two Roríguez homes. We even learned that he was to blame for the raid last week at Emerald Club."

"Brazen."

"That's what you called it a week ago. Your description got me thinking."

"What does this mean for the alliance?" I asked with more than a little fear at the thought of losing what we'd accomplished.

Dante scoffed. "*El Patrón's* number-one son is currently spending the night in the capo dei capi's home. I'd have to say that the Luciano/Roríguez alliance is solid."

I ran my palm over his hard shoulder and down his muscular arm. "I'm very glad to hear that. I'm rather fond of the Luciano/Ruiz alliance we have going."

"You're now a Luciano. You're famiglia."

Before I could comment, Dante's lips seized mine.

The warmth within me multiplied as Dante pressed his solid chest over my breasts, my nipples beading against the satin and lace of my nightgown. Parting my lips, I allowed his tongue entry, their dance teasing my tastebuds with minty freshness as his roaming touch moved lower.

Dante stilled. "If you're too sore..."

Lifting my hand to his smooth cheek, I grinned. "You shaved too."

"I did."

"I'm not too sore. The bath and muscle relaxers helped. I want this. I crave being close to you. You make me feel safe and loved."

"You're fucking safe and loved, Camila. Never doubt that."

"I didn't. Even when I woke in that truck, I knew you'd do whatever you could to save me."

I sat up as Dante lifted the hem of my nightgown. Wiggling, I helped as he pulled the soft material over my head. His touch roamed, gently and reverently, over my skin as if he too needed reassurance of my safety and our connection. Kisses rained down as the air filled with his praises and promises accompanied by my chorus of hums of pleasure.

Endorphins flooded my circulation as I became lost to the deep baritone timbre of his voice and the omnipresent feel of his body against mine. Ambers within me caught fire, stoked by Dante's pursuit to bring me pleasure. Sparks ignited as he kissed and sucked my breasts, leaving my nipples diamond hard and goose bumps in his wake.

It was as he teased my folds, finding me wet and ready, that the combustion reached record temperatures, sizzling and scorching as he pressed within me.

"Those muscle relaxers must not be working," he said with his warm breath teasing the sensitive skin near my ear. "You're so fucking tight." He brought his nose to mine. "No one touches you and lives to talk about it. Do you understand?"

I nodded. "I'm yours, Dante."

My back arched as he pressed his length within. There was something different in his movements, something slower and yet deliberate. This wasn't fucking. This was making love and keeping his promise. The night passed slowly and tenderly, our mutual need for closeness resulting in multiple sessions of lovemaking. We'd fall asleep in one another's arms to be awakened by the other's affection.

Sometime before dawn, I awoke to his tongue lapping my core. My orgasm was so intense and powerful that if not for the full-body convulsions and his iron grip of my hips, I might have thought it was a dream. As the sun rose, I found us spooning, my back to his front, and his arms encasing me, protecting me.

A wiggle of my behind and I was acutely aware of his hard cock seeking entrance from behind. I moaned at the filling sensation of him once again within me. Slow and luxurious thrusts combined with his attention to my breasts and clit sent fireworks exploding behind my closed eyelids. Dante continued as my body languished in satiation. His guttural roar reverberated deep in his chest and echoed off the walls as he found his release.

Breaking our union, I rolled until his dark brown orbs dominated my sight. "What happens now?"

"Aléjandro is going to take Mia and Valentina back to San Diego. Silas has neutralized the threat next door."

"What about Herrera?"

"Aléjandro and Reinaldo are going to consult with Jorge." He inhaled. "Jorge and Dario will have the final words in the decisions, but if the Roríguez cartel is at war with the Herrera cartel, they're not in it alone."

EPILOGUE

Camila
Three months later

I hurried from the bed to the window. "It's snowing."

"It does that in the winter, beautiful."

A blanket of white coated the world beyond our window as large flakes filtered down from the clouds above. "It makes me think of skiing."

Dante pulled back the blankets and patted the mattress. "It makes me think of cold. Come back to bed and let me warm you."

Doing as he said, I walked back to the bed and crawled under the blankets. With a push of a button on the remote, Dante brought the fireplace to life.

I curled against his side, my head on my favorite pillow, that of his rock-hard shoulder. "I've enjoyed the time off, but I'm ready to get back to my classes at Missouri State-Kansas City after the first of the year."

"You'll be the sophomore with the big guy following her everywhere she goes."

"I like Giovanni. He doesn't hover."

Dante kissed my hair. "I trust him, not just with protecting you, but also respecting you."

I nodded. "My parents will be here later today for the holiday."

Em, Rei, Aléjandro, and Mia were already in Kansas City. It was going to be an old-fashioned holiday, the kind where the cartel and Mafia break bread.

At the ding of a text message, Dante rolled and lifted his phone. "Oh, your present is about to arrive."

"My present? We said no gifts."

His sexy smile grew. "What can I say? I'm a criminal by nature. Sometimes I'm not one hundred percent forthcoming."

"You'd lie to me?" I asked, aghast.

"Only to surprise you."

Excitement electrified my circulation. "What are you going to surprise me with?"

He rolled from the bed, standing in all his Greek-god glory. Michelangelo's David had nothing on Dante Luciano. "Since your sister is delivering it in a few minutes, I suggest we put on some clothes."

"Cat's bringing my present."

Dante laughed as he stepped into his boxer briefs. "That's more accurate than you know."

I furrowed my forehead. "I don't understand."

He lifted my nightgown from the floor. "You might want this."

Getting out of bed, I went to him and took the satin gown. Pushing myself up to my tiptoes, I brushed his lips with mine. "I don't know why I waste money on nightgowns; somehow, they always seem to get lost during the night."

"You have them to answer the door in the morning." Excitement shone in his eyes. "Come on, hurry."

I quickly hurried to the bathroom, took care of business, splashed water on my face and ran my toothbrush over my teeth. Once I was dressed in panties, nightgown, and robe, I combed my long hair, securing it behind my head in a low ponytail.

As I exited our bedroom, I heard voices coming from our kitchen. When I turned the corner to find not only Cat, but also Dario holding Ariadna Gia, and Jasmine—also visiting for the holiday—I was glad I'd taken the time to add panties and a robe. "Good morning."

"Good morning," came from all around.

Dante was standing shirtless with his legs covered by blue jeans. He grinned like a cat who swallowed a canary.

My fists went to my hips. "Are you all in on this surprise?"

"Yes," Dante, Cat, and Jasmine answered as Dario nodded.

Ariadna Gia smiled as if she too was in on the surprise.

"Well, I'd offer you coffee, but first I want to know what you're all so happy about."

Dante leaned down. He stood back up, squaring his shoulders at the sound of the elevator. I watched his expressions change and the way his jaw set. Dario handed his daughter to Cat, seconds before we all sighed with relief.

Em and Rei stepped off, looking like killers who had just woken up.

"Where's the coffee?" my brother asked.

"You have to wait for my surprise," I replied.

Rei and Em both stopped when their gaze landed on the red-headed beauty at Cat's side.

"You two know Jasmine?" Dante said.

"They do. I'm waiting here," I prompted.

Dante's shit-eating grin was back as he leaned down and lifted a box to the counter. The box had a handle and large holes.

My mind was scrambling with what could be inside when I heard the mew.

Tears filled my eyes. "You got me a kitten?" I rushed to the box, opening it to the sweetest green stare and tiny body covered with multicolored fluffy fur. The purring began as soon as I lifted the tiny kitten to my chest. My gaze met Dante's. "How did you know? We never talked about pets."

He rubbed the kitten's head and kissed my cheek. "One of our soldiers took in a pregnant stray—more accurately, his wife did. The timing was too perfect."

Hugging the kitten, my emotions overtook me. I smiled up at my husband with fresh tears in my eyes. "I've always wanted a cat." I spun toward my brother and sister. "Remember Bell?"

Cat nodded with a grin.

"Catalina," Dante said, "told me that story when you were missing."

"Oh." My eyes opened wide. "My passcode."

Dante nodded. "I promised you to make your dreams come true. I have about fifty years to work on more."

"What are you going to name her?" Jasmine asked, coming closer to the kitten.

Ignoring the sideway glances Dario was shooting toward Em and Rei, I looked over to Dante. "Do you have an idea?"

"That's up to you, beautiful."

I held the kitten up, staring into her round eyes. "What's your name, little one?"

"She's a girl," Cat said. "Just thought you should know that."

My wedding ring caught my eye. The large ruby on the gold band now had an accompanying diamond encrusted band. "Her name is Diamond because she shines."

Dante leaned down. "Welcome to the famiglia, Diamond." He extended his hands, and I laid Diamond in his grasp. "Don't pee on me."

I wrapped my arms around my husband's torso and squeezed. "I love you."

"I love you back."

There was no doubt, looking from Dario, Cat, Ariadna Gia, and Jasmine, to Dante, Em, Rei, Diamond, and me that this alliance was strong. We'd been through rough patches. We all knew that despite the love and unions within our individual couples, we'd need to unite as one to take on the future.

If you don't want the BRUTAL VOWS series to end, get ready for QUEENS AND MONSTERS featuring all our beloved couples and a surprise new one as the Luciano famiglia and the Roríguez cartel battle a dangerous common enemy.
Coming in 2025.

Thank you for reading BOUND BY A PROMISE, Dante and Camila's story. If you haven't read Dario and Catalina's story, check out NOW AND FOREVER. Aléjandro and Mia's story is TILL DEATH DO US PART.

What to do now

LEND IT: Did you enjoy Bound by a Promise? Do you have a friend who'd enjoy Bound by a Promise? Bound by a Promise may be lent one time. Sharing is caring!

RECOMMEND IT: Do you have multiple friends who'd enjoy Bound by a Promise? Tell them about it! Call, text, post, tweet...your recommendation is the nicest gift you can give to an author!

REVIEW IT: Tell the world. Please go to the retailer where you purchased this book, as well as Goodreads, and write a review. Please share your thoughts about Bound by a PromiseS on:

*Amazon, Bound by a Promise, Customer Reviews

*Barnes & Noble, Bound by a Promise, Customer Reviews

*iBooks, Bound by a Promise, Customer Reviews

*Goodreads.com/Aleatha Romig

Books by ALEATHA

BRUTAL VOWS:

NOW AND FOREVER

May 2024

TILL DEATH DO US PART

June 2024

BOUND BY A PROMISE

October 2024

QUEENS AND MONSTERS

2025

READY TO BINGE

SINCLAIR DUET:

REMEMBERING PASSION

September 2023

REKINDLING DESIRE

October 2023

ROYAL REFLECTIONS SERIES:

RUTHLESS REIGN

November 2022

RESILIENT REIGN

January 2023

RAVISHING REIGN

April 2023

RELEVANT REIGN

June 2023

SIN SERIES:

RED SIN

October 2021

GREEN ENVY

January 2022

GOLD LUST

April 2022

BLACK KNIGHT

June 2022

STAND-ALONE ROMANTIC SUSPENSE:

SILVER LINING

October 2022

KINGDOM COME

November 2021

DEVIL'S SERIES (Duet):

DEVIL'S DEAL

May 2021

ANGEL'S PROMISE

June 2021

WEB OF SIN:

SECRETS

October 2018

LIES

December 2018

PROMISES

January 2019

TANGLED WEB:

TWISTED

May 2019

OBSESSED

July 2019

BOUND

August 2019

WEB OF DESIRE:

SPARK

Jan. 14, 2020

FLAME

February 25, 2020

ASHES

April 7, 2020

DANGEROUS WEB:

Prequel: "Danger's First Kiss"

DUSK

November 2020

DARK

January 2021

DAWN

February 2021

THE INFIDELITY SERIES:

BETRAYAL

Book #1

October 2015

CUNNING

Book #2

January 2016

DECEPTION

Book #3

May 2016

ENTRAPMENT

Book #4

September 2016

FIDELITY

Book #5

January 2017

THE CONSEQUENCES SERIES:

CONSEQUENCES

(Book #1)

August 2011

TRUTH

(Book #2)

October 2012

CONVICTED

(Book #3)

October 2013

REVEALED

(Book #4)

Previously titled: Behind His Eyes Convicted: The Missing Years

June 2014

BEYOND THE CONSEQUENCES

(Book #5)

January 2015

RIPPLES (Consequences stand-alone)

October 2017

CONSEQUENCES COMPANION READS:

BEHIND HIS EYES-CONSEQUENCES

January 2014

BEHIND HIS EYES-TRUTH

March 2014

∼

STAND ALONE MAFIA THRILLER:

PRICE OF HONOR

Available Now

∼

STAND-ALONE ROMANTIC THRILLER:

ON THE EDGE

May 2022

***

TALES FROM THE DARK SIDE SERIES:

INSIDIOUS

(All books in this series are stand-alone erotic thrillers)

Released October 2014

~

ALEATHA'S LIGHTER ONES:

PLUS ONE

Stand-alone fun, sexy romance

May 2017

ANOTHER ONE

Stand-alone fun, sexy romance

May 2018

ONE NIGHT

Stand-alone, sexy contemporary romance

September 2017

A SECRET ONE

April 2018

MY ALWAYS ONE

Stand-Alone, sexy friends to lovers contemporary romance

July 2021

QUINTESSENTIALLY THE ONE

Stand-alone, small-town, second-chance, secret baby
contemporary romance

July 2022

ONE KISS

Stand-alone, small-town, best friend's sister, grump/sunshine contemporary romance.

July 2023

ONE STRING

Second-chance, enemies-to-lovers, fake-date, little-sister's-best-friend, forbidden, stand-alone contemporary romance

July 2024

INDULGENCE SERIES:

UNEXPECTED

August 2018

UNCONVENTIONAL

January 2018

UNFORGETTABLE

October 2019

UNDENIABLE

August 2020

ABOUT THE AUTHOR

Aleatha Romig is a New York Times, Wall Street Journal, and USA Today bestselling author who lives in Indiana, USA. She grew up in Mishawaka, graduated from Indiana University, and is currently living south of Indianapolis. Aleatha has raised three children with her high school sweetheart and husband of nearly thirty years. Before she became a full-time author, she worked days as a dental hygienist and spent her nights writing. Now, when she's not imagining mind-blowing twists and turns, she likes to spend her time a with her family and friends. Her other pastimes include reading and creating heroes/anti-heroes who haunt your dreams!

Aleatha released her first novel, CONSEQUENCES, in August of 2011. CONSEQUENCES became a bestselling series with five novels and two companions released from 2011 through 2015. The compelling and epic story of Anthony and Claire Rawlings has graced more than half a million e-readers. Aleatha released the first of her series TALES FROM THE DARK SIDE, INSIDIOUS, in the fall of 2014. These stand alone thrillers continue Aleatha's twisted style with an increase in heat.

In the fall of 2015, Aleatha moved head first into the world of dark romantic suspense with the release of BETRAYAL, the first of her five novel INFIDELITY series that has taken the reading world by storm. She also began her traditional publishing career with Thomas and Mercer. Her books INTO THE LIGHT and AWAY FROM THE DARK were published through this mystery/thriller publisher in 2016.

2017 brings Aleatha's first "Leatha, the lighter side of Aleatha" with PLUS ONE, a fun, sexy romantic comedy.

Aleatha is a "Published Author's Network" member of the Romance Writers of America and PEN America. She is represented by Kevan Lyon of Marsal Lyon Literary Agency.

Stay connected with Aleatha

Do you love Aleatha's writing? Do you want to keep up to date about what's coming next?

Do you like EXCLUSIVE content (never-released scenes, never-released excerpts, and more)? Would you like the monthly chance to win prizes (signed books and gift cards)? Then sign up today for Aleatha's monthly newsletter and stay informed on all things Aleatha Romig.

NEWSLETTER: Recipients of Aleatha's Newsletter receive exclusive material and offers.

Aleatha's Newsletter Sign-up

You can also find Aleatha@

Goodreads: http://www.goodreads.com/author/show/5131072.Aleatha_Romig

Instagram: http://instagram.com/aleatharomig

You may also listen to Aleatha Romig books on Audible:

http://www.audible.com/search/ref=a_mn_mt_ano_t seft_galileo?advsearchKeywords=aleatha+romig&spre fixRefmarker=nb_sb_ss_i_0_7&sprefix=aleatha

www.aleatharomig.com
aleatharomig@gmail.com

 X